KU-102-693

TOMB OF THE SERPENT

Superintendent Henry Jarrett thinks he has encountered murder in all its forms, but gory human sacrifice is horribly new. Is there a madman loose in Victorian Glasgow, as Jarrett, Inspector Grant and Sergeant Quinn believe? The victims are randomly chosen, the killings unpredictable and thus unsolvable. Then, a murder at a travelling fair — which bears no resemblance to the others — and the little matter of the valuable artefacts, increases Jarrett's confusion. It seems the time is right for him to tie the knot with his beloved Elsie Maitland and retire to the seaside — before his chief constable demands his resignation.

Books by Guy Fraser
Published by The House of Ulverscroft:

BLADE OF THE ASSASSIN
JUPITER'S GOLD
A PLAGUE OF LIONS
AVENGING THE DEAD

B52 003 795 X

SPECIAL MESSAGE TO READERS

This book is published under the auspices of

THE ULVERSCROFT FOUNDATION

(registered charity No. 264873 UK)

Established in 1972 to provide funds for
ses.

ROTHERHAM LIBRARY & INFORMATION SERVICE

BRINSWORTH

9\18

DINNINGTON

11/19

DIN

16

s.

ren,

ion
ery
d

sue as

he) for

LIS7b

uoting

the above number / author / title.

Enquiries: 01709 336774

www.rotherham.gov.uk/libraries

nd

94-98 Chalmers Street, Surry Hills,
N.S.W. 2010, Australia

Guy Fraser was born in Scotland and has an MA in Ancient History and Classical Archaeology from Edinburgh University. His previous novels include *A Plague of Lions, Jupiter's Gold* and *Blade of the Assassin*.

GUY FRASER

TOMB OF THE SERPENT

Complete and Unabridged

ULVERSCROFT
Leicester

First published in Great Britain in 2011 by
Robert Hale Limited
London

First Large Print Edition
published 2012
by arrangement with
Robert Hale Limited
London

The moral right of the author has been asserted

Copyright © 2011 by Guy Fraser
All rights reserved

British Library CIP Data

Fraser, Guy.
    Tomb of the serpent.
    1. Serial murder investigation- -Scotland- -Glasgow- -
    Fiction. 2. Police- -Scotland- -Glasgow- -Fiction.
    3. Glasgow (Scotland)- -Social life and customs- -
    19th century- -Fiction. 4. Detective and mystery
    stories. 5. Large type books.
    I. Title
    823.9'2–dc23

    ISBN 978–1–4448–1135–3

ROTHERHAM LIBRARY &
INFORMATION SERVICES

B52003795X

OES4b3952

Published by
F. A. Thorpe (Publishing)
Anstey, Leicestershire

Set by Words & Graphics Ltd.
Anstey, Leicestershire
Printed and bound in Great Britain by
T. J. International Ltd., Padstow, Cornwall

This book is printed on acid-free paper

The History

1745

They sat well back from the glowing brazier, patiently awaiting some proof that out there in the darkness a friendly vessel from a far-off land had entered this perilous bay and was now lying at anchor.

In all probability, the Spanish captain of the *Nuestra Señora de Cartagena* was unfamiliar with these waters and would be disinclined to accept the onshore light as friendly. It might well be the prearranged signal, but equally it could be a wreckers' fire or a Hanoverian trap. Only when he was reasonably secure in his mind that all was well would those waiting silently on the shingle beach hear the first, distant lapping of oars.

But the watchers were themselves being watched. Deeper in the darkness, others who had no sympathy with the cause, listened, daggers at the ready, for the coming of the long-boats. Then, without word or sound, they crept forward, one man to one man, hands clasped over mouths and knives driven between ribs, before dragging the lifeless victims back into the blackest shadows and taking their places as the sea watchers.

At first, only one of the boats made landfall. Two sailors leapt over the gunwales and, when they were not cut down by a volley of government muskets, were joined by two companions. As they swiftly unloaded the boxes and placed them on the moist pebbles, a second long-boat ground onto the shale and its crew disposed of their cargo in similar fashion. Since there was no common tongue between the seamen and those waiting on the shore, the Spaniards pushed their boats back into the water, jumped on board and began to recede into the murk until not even the sound of their oars could compete with the snapping and cracking of the dry twigs in the brazier.

There were eight boxes in all. One by one, they were carried up the slope to the rough path on which sat a flat-bed wagon. When the last of the chests was safely stowed and the whole covered with a coarse cotton sheet, the driver's companion distributed the leather bags of silver which were the agreed payment for the night's work. What was in the boxes, or where they were bound was of no interest to the ambushers who guessed correctly that they could not dispose of the contents easily and would wind up on the gallows if they tried.

* * *

The west wing of the big house was old. Prior to the building of the main property and the matching east wing, it was little more than a medieval keep, set high on the slopes above the gorge and its fast-moving river. According to local legend, it had been the retreat of an important churchman before the Reformation. Now it was very probably the finest of all the mansions in the Vale.

It was not easily accessible, though; apart from the narrow track through the thick woods, there was no easy way in. But the path, such as it was, allowed the master and his servant to bring the flat-bed wagon close to the former tower.

And they did so unobserved. Most of the staff had been sent down to their master's summer residence on the estuary, with only the cook and a kitchen girl being kept back to attend to his immediate needs. At this hour even they would be asleep in their attic room to the rear of the house. They might as well have been a million miles away.

The original west wing had no foundations as such, but did boast a bottle dungeon beneath the large stone slab immediately in front of the great hearth. No doubt the sufferings of those poor devils who had fallen foul of the bishop of the time would be further aggravated by the aroma of spit-turned meat.

After travelling for almost two days and one night, stopping only to give the horses a nosebag and a rest, it took the master and his servant most of the second night to lower all eight chests into the pit. Doing this took them to the limit of their combined strength. Then, while the servant stood by with a bright oil lamp, his master set about opening the first box.

There was only one key for all the locks. It protruded from an ornate keyhole plate and required a considerable amount of pressure to turn it. Rather than using external padlocks, which were easy to break with a mallet and cold steel chisel, the Spaniards preferred vertical locks fitted inside the chests. When the key was turned the double tongues spread apart and engaged the keepers in the lid.

The goods within the box were unlike anything the simple and superstitious servant had ever seen, or could begin to imagine. They were the devil's work, images of evil creatures and contorted humans straight from the very bowels of hell itself. He watched in horror as his master undid the woven wrapping from one abomination after another and examined each with unashamed glee.

'Wonderful,' the master whispered hoarsely as he peeled away a small bulrush mat and exposed a green jaguar not much longer than his hand. He was not addressing his servant, however, as the man did not matter one jot in the scheme of things. 'Such craftsmanship, such artistry. Even more magnificent than I dared to hope.'

'Will you let the minister see it?' the servant asked, his voice wavering.

The master snorted.

'He is an old fool,' he said. 'You're nothing but timid goats, the pair of you.'

'But he's the minister.'

'And an ignorant man. It was stupid creatures like him who destroyed countless thousands of such beautiful objects. Different nation, different religion, but the same mindless terror of the unknown. Why should I consult him when he wouldn't even know what he was looking at?'

'Well, sir,' the servant said, placing the lamp on the dungeon floor, 'you may do as you wish, but I intend to save my eternal soul from the likes of that.'

The master returned the crouching cat to the chest and lifted a wooden-shafted club instead. After so long he would have expected the timber to have rotted away, but this had not and he suspected that they might have been recently replaced. Still, it was of no matter. It was the ornate head that was all-important.

He turned then, his mind made up, and saw his servant scrambling desperately up the ladder, his nerves rent asunder and his words tumbling insanely from his lips.

'Come back here, you fool!' the master shouted angrily. 'Do as I say now!'

But the man's wits had deserted him and he was in the grip of religious terror. All that mattered to him was keeping out of the clutches of Old Nick himself.

The master chased the panic-stricken servant for a considerable distance along the stony, shrub-edged path, trying from time to time to bring him down with the mighty war club, but always missing by a mere hand's width, until the pursuer managed that extra few desperate inches and brought the mace-like ball down on the left shoulder of his quarry. Instantly, the servant stumbled forward and landed on both knees. The second and final blow was to the top of the head, killing him instantly.

For half a minute or so the master hovered above the corpse, his thoughts tumbling wildly as he tried to come to terms with the enormity of his crime. Sending countless sailors to their deaths in heavily insured coffin ships was one thing, as was the hiring of common thugs to stick the men on the beach, but this was entirely different. It was the first time he had personally killed a man.

He considered tipping the body over the edge of the gorge and letting it tumble down into the river, but it would probably be found quite quickly and a hue and cry raised. His next idea was to fetch a spade and bury the remains in the woods where they might never be found. Once that was done, he thought, he would return the weapon to its iron-bound chest and slide the large hearthstone back into place over the bottle dungeon. After that, he would arouse the cook and the girl from their slumbers and instruct them to prepare a meal for him, the first in days.

1

1863

Upon descending the stairs and entering the dining parlour of Mrs Maitland's superior guest-house for single gentlemen, Superintendent Henry Jarrett of the Detective Department at Glasgow Central acknowledged the other three occupants with a curt nod of the head. There was no definite rule regarding talking; it was simply an unwritten law observed by all, except Albert Sweetman, travelling partner at Hall & Sweetman, who felt in his portly and colourful way somehow obliged to entertain everyone with whom he came into contact. No one else felt this compulsion, neither the quiet and unassuming chemist, Wilbur McConnell, nor Elliot Stainer, the most recent arrival at number 76 and a salaried officer of the Clyde Navigation Trust, nor even Henry Jarrett himself.

Of medium height and uncertain age, the clean-shaven Jarrett could have been accused of being unremarkable, yet somehow he exuded an air of authority. This he had acquired and finely honed during his time with the Hong Kong police.

But it was here at Elsie Maitland's excellent establishment, and at breakfast primarily, that Jarrett's firm and long-established ways could be most easily observed by interested parties. For example, he had no truck with conventional teas and coffees, preferring instead Iron Goddess of Mercy — Ti Kuan Yin — which in his estimation was the finest of the Black Dragon teas. To ensure a constant supply, he would regularly collect a pound of the leaf from McKillop the China tea importer and present it to Mrs Maitland, who had long since learnt that it must be infused in hot water, never boiling. Jarrett's only other unwavering requirement was thickly cut, golden brown toast, which had to be buttered to the edges and accompanied by a pot of Keiller's marmalade. Otherwise, he was really quite easy-going.

For example, there was no question of his insisting that the dining-area should be a no-smoking area. He merely let it be known that he preferred it that way, and for some strange reason it became so. Also, he had long since discovered that by the simple expedient of producing his silver hunter, springing it open and consulting it with a pronounced frown, even the loquacious Albert Sweetman fell silent and huddled over his meal like a burrowing ant-eater.

To date, Jarrett was a bachelor, entirely set in his ways yet not unyielding. Certainly, no one else was allowed to polish his boots, or clean the windows of his Wardian case, which housed a variety of small ferns, from the oak fern, soft shield, hart's tongue to the rock brake and parsley fern, all protected behind glass from the coal smoke and sulphuric acid of Glasgow's air.

On this particular occasion the usual restriction on talk was not in force, and comments came fast and furious from all four corners of the dining room. The subject, of course, was the weather. For three days and nights it had rained incessantly, turning the riverside streets into canals. The water level in the Clyde had risen to such an extent that sailing-ships stood high along the Broomielaw like a wall of black timber. Moreover, they found it difficult, if not impossible, to leave their berths and make for the open sea. For with the rushing water had come hundreds of tons of silt from the hills to clog this waterway and make it impassable as it had not done for a long time.

It was only through the constant efforts of the steam-driven dredgers that vessels from distant parts could come this far up river, yet

10

they were now being stretched to their very limit. And no one knew that better than the man from the Clyde Navigation Trust, Elliot Stainer.

'At least the rain has stopped now,' Stainer said in answer to a complaint from Sweetman. 'The truth is, I don't have enough dredgers. I could use two more and extra hoppers for dumping the sludge out in deep water.'

'All I know,' the salesman went on, 'is that I should have set off on my selling and collecting tour of the Hebrides two days ago, but the steamboat captains refuse to budge. Unfortunately, the senior partner, Mr Hall, is not an understanding man in any sense of the word. I am now going to have to do a five day trip in three days.'

'We all have our crosses to bear,' chemist Wilbur McConnell offered. 'Even though the water in my shop will have subsided by now, it is going to take a considerable amount of cleaning. They say I will get no insurance money because it is an act of God.'

Henry Jarrett listened to their complaining for a few moments.

'Well, gentlemen,' he said with a smile, 'it is an old adage that rain is the best policeman. Burglars don't come out in it, and drinkers scurry homewards rather than become involved in brawls. But of course such benefits are offset by the fact that we are faced with the identification of a greater than usual number of corpses taken from the swollen river by George Geddes of the Humane Society.'

'Well, I don't know about the corpses,' Albert Sweetman offered, 'but I think you ought to make use of the rogues who are supposed to be doing hard labour in Duke Street prison. What is the use of having them walk the wheel or picking oakum when they could be out in chains, sweeping the gutters?'

'Not up to me, I'm afraid,' Jarrett said, consulting his watch. In just six minutes the Menzies tartan bus would depart from its western terminus. 'However, it may come to that. Only time will tell.'

★　★　★

About then steam Dredger four was clearing the river at Pointhouse so that the new side-paddler, *Duchess of Oban*, could be launched by the lady of that same name later in the forenoon. Crewman Billy Gregg, who was positioned forward on the vessel to keep an eye on the endless chain of iron buckets, raised an arm to let Captain Dan Mason know that they had scooped up more than

12

mere silt. Since stopping the process was both time-wasting and costly, Mason waited until that particular bucket had deposited its load into the hopper before taking the appropriate action. A corpse would by law have necessitated halting the dredging, but anything else called for a snap decision. Then old Gus McIvor threw a pail of water over the chunky object and exposed it as an iron-bound box.

'Bloody hell!' Dan Mason shouted over the din, and hauled on the lever to stop the chain. 'Get it out of there!'

Using a long-shafted boat hook, Gus McIvor managed to engage one of the box's oval handles, and between them he and young Billy managed to pull it out of the sticky mud, over the gunwale and onto the deck of the dredger.

'What do you think, Gaffer?' Billy asked, grinning. 'Reckon it's worth a bit?'

'If it is, the Trust'll have it. We'll be lucky to get ten bob and a kick in the arse.'

'Probably not worth much more than that, anyway,' Billy suggested. 'Looks like a seaman's chest.'

Old Gus shook his head emphatically.

'Too small,' he declared. 'The one I had was twice as big.'

'Makes no difference what it is.' Dan

Mason released the lever and set the bucket chain in motion once more. 'I'll tell them about it after the shift. Right now we'd better get a move on, or we'll have one of them down here to find out why we've stopped.'

* * *

Elliot Stainer, new fellow at Mrs Maitland's guest-house, was perhaps not the last person Henry Jarrett expected to encounter that forenoon, but he was certainly one of them.

The first police officer on the scene was PS Raymond MacLeish, who declined to accept responsibility for the wooden chest, but suggested that it be moved away from the quay and relocated in the yard behind the Clyde Navigation Trust building. Likewise, Detective Sergeant Tommy Quinn considered himself to be less than qualified to determine the fate of the object, preferring instead to defer to his superiors. Unfortunately, Superintendent Henry Jarrett and Inspector Charlie Grant were equally vague on the subject of trove.

The problem was Scottish Law's definition of treasure. Whereas in England gold and silver in plate or coin, if found beneath the ground, is the property of the Crown, in Scotland everything that could be shown to be of historic value and yet ownerless fell into that category.

With PC Jamieson as always at the ribbons, and Domino happily between the shafts, the wagonette sped along the cobbled Broomielaw until it reached the most imposing building on the waterfront. The domed Clyde Navigation Trust Building was in an Italianate Baroque style, and the facade decoration showed Father Clyde, enthroned, alongside statues of Poseidon, Triton, Demeter and Amphitrite, while below stood statues of Thomas Telford, James Watt and Henry Bell.

When the wagonette emerged from the lane at the side of the building, Jarrett and Grant were dismayed to see Chief Constable Rattray's chariot dominating the yard. The CC himself was holding an animated conversation with Elliot Stainer and two other officers of the Clyde Navigation Trust. In the circumstances this was to be expected; the unpaid directors of the Trust were his kind of people — city fathers, shipbuilders, merchants and industrialists — so it would have been out of character for him not to put in an appearance to assure the Trust officers that their claim for the full reward would be given priority. And all this without knowing what, if anything, was inside the chest.

Superintendent Jarrett's sudden appearance was clearly unwelcome, as it threatened their cosy little arrangements.

'Who or what is that?' Rattray demanded, levelling his cane at the third man who stepped down from the wagonette.

'This, Chief Constable,' Henry Jarrett replied amicably, 'is Donald Wylie, lock-pick and common thief, who specialises in stealing from embarking passengers' trunks.'

'Then why is he walking around free? Why isn't he in irons?'

'Mainly because we can't prove anything, sir. The injured parties tend to be on the high seas before they find out that they have lost their silver.'

Rattray closed in on Jarrett, his complexion deepening by the second.

'You listen to me, Jarrett,' he growled. 'If you are trying to humiliate me — '

'I am trying to do no such thing, sir. Wylie is here because he is the only man I know who can open the chest without causing criminal damage.'

The Chief Constable continued to glare at him for a few moments, then turned away abruptly and waved his cane like a wand.

'Proceed,' he snapped. 'And have him be quick about it.'

Wylie first stooped over the box, closely

examining the wood and the type of joint used in its construction. Even now what remained of the river water was seeping out between two or three of the tight-fitting planks. But the flow was weak and almost finished.

'Camphorwood,' he said at length.

'What the hell has that got to do with anything?' Rattray demanded.

'I'm reading the box,' Donald Wylie answered, glancing over his shoulder. 'Do you want to know about it or not?'

'Tell us,' Jarrett put in quickly, 'if you think it is relevant.'

'That's up to you, Superintendent. I'll tell you its story and you can decide if it matters.'

'Then carry on.'

'Well, as I say it's camphorwood. At least two centuries old. The joints and the ironwork are Spanish. For most of its life it has been in a nice, dry place, and only recently ended up in the water.'

'How recently?'

'A few days, I'd say. Two or three at the most.'

Rattray, who had been barely able to contain his exasperation, finally exploded.

'What bloody nonsense!' he yelled. 'How in the name of God could this petty rogue know these things?'

'Because it's my trade,' Wylie said through his teeth.

'You don't have a trade. You are a low nasty thief.'

Jarrett sensed that Wylie was about to make the biggest mistake of his life and placed a hand on the man's shoulder to defuse the situation.

'Open the chest,' he said flatly.

Wylie produced his bunch of picks and selected the one he judged to be closest to the height of the fancy keyhole. But Chief Constable Rattray had not quite finished.

'I trust you intend to confiscate those things, Jarrett,' he snapped. 'Indeed, I should have thought that possession of such tools was cause enough for arrest and punishment.'

'With all due respect, sir,' said Henry Jarrett, 'every locksmith in the land keeps skeleton keys and a set of picks. It isn't illegal. People lose their keys regularly.'

After waiting a few moments for Rattray to respond to this, but hearing nothing, Donald Wylie set to work. In less than two minutes there came the satisfying sound of double iron tongues disengaging from their keepers.

'I told you it hadn't been under the water for long,' he said, rising to his feet. 'Nothing clogging it and no rust.'

But as Wylie made to lift the lid Rattray

stepped forward and pressed down heavily on it with his cane.

'That will do,' he ordered. 'Withdraw to an appropriate distance.'

Having been promised a run home and half a crown for his troubles, Wylie grumbled his way over to the wagonette and waited patiently, while Henry Jarrett lifted the chest lid and the others crowded around.

At first sight the contents were disappointing, and appeared to be comprised of extremely wet rolls of rush mats. The superintendent lifted one and discovered that it had been used as wrapping, perhaps to protect the item within from the buffeting it would receive on the open seas.

When the fifth winding had been undone all parties present stood fixed to the spot, their expectations confounded. The thing now exposed was a man-sized mask of translucent green with long, white fangs and a strange design on its forehead.

'Good God!' Rattray uttered softly. 'What on earth is it?'

'A jade mask,' Henry Jarrett said.

'Ugly damned thing. Is it worth anything?'

'If you were in China right now you could name your own price.'

'Oh yes, I forgot. You are an expert on all things Chinese.'

19

Jarrett ignored this sarcastic remark.

'If you live in China for any length of time,' he said, 'you soon learn about jade, the good and the bad. The best of it is more valuable than gold or silver.'

'So you are saying that this is Chinese?'

'No, sir, it certainly isn't that.'

'Then what? Stopping talking in riddles, man.'

Henry Jarrett took a deep breath and refused to permit Rattray to provoke him.

'Possibly the New World,' he said, calmly spacing his words.

'I hardly think so. I have read extensively about the American Indians and this is assuredly not their work.'

'I was thinking more of Central America, Chief Constable. Mexico, perhaps. After all the chest is most likely Spanish.'

'And you are most likely guessing, Superintendent Jarrett.'

'Yes, I am, sir. All I can say for certain is that it is blue green jade of the highest quality. In China this could make you a very rich man indeed.'

'Then we must see what else there is,' Rattray said curtly. 'Unwrap another object.'

Jarrett handed the moist reed package and its valuable charge to Inspector Grant, who looked down at it in dismay.

'But I'm a bit clumsy,' Charlie Grant objected softy.

'You had better not be, or you'll be back on the beat,' Jarrett warned. 'In Inverness.'

The second item was not jade but gold. It was a turtle and it bore a similar design to the mask.

'Now that is something I can appreciate,' the Chief Constable declared. 'What I want you to do, Jarrett, is return these objects to the chest and hand the whole lot over to these officers of the Clyde Navigation Trust.'

'There is an alternative to that, sir,' Henry Jarrett pointed out. 'We could make the box secure with a chain and padlock and transport it to Sergeant Black's lost property store, where it will be held in the secure cage.'

Rattray closed in on the superintendent.

'I gave you an order,' he snarled.

'And I give you the law,' Jarrett retorted. 'We have established that the chest has not been long in the water. To me that suggests that it is not ownerless.'

'Do you want to face the Police Commission?'

'Do you want to face theft by finding?'

For a full minute Rattray tried to stare down the superintendent, then he suddenly spun on his heel and made angrily for his coach. As he strode past Elliot Stainer and his assistant he yelled, 'The man is impossible, completely impossible. I'll see him finished yet.'

Stainer, evidently displeased, also quit the scene and, followed by the lesser clerk, withdrew to the Trust building. But in his case not a word was spoken.

'I don't think we are going to get this on to the wagonette,' Henry Jarrett said. Then, while Charlie Grant gingerly returned the artefacts to their rightful places within the chest, turned his attention to Tommy Quinn. 'Consign it to the lost property lock-up, Sergeant, then I want you to take a photograph of the jade mask and bring me a print. After you have done that we will make an inventory of the full contents of the chest. When we have finished we must secure the box with a chain and padlock, as I said, and make sure than no one but the three of us has access to it.'

'Not even . . . '

'No one, Sergeant Quinn.'

2

The arrival of Boscombe's Travelling Fair
had been eagerly anticipated for a month or
more. Very few ordinary people, if any, would
not have been seduced by the colourful
posters that were plastered over many
previously blank walls or scattered liberally
on the seats of the numerous horse-buses.
Only the better-off, who generally considered
the whole thing to be base and criminal, and
the police for whom it always meant extra
work, were opposed to their coming. But
there was nothing they could do to prevent
it. What they could do, however, was contain
them in Glasgow Green. Thanks to the
recent Act, which gave control of the streets
to the police, the showmen were no longer at
liberty to erect their tents and stalls in the
Saltmarket, Trongate and Broomielaw, where
the milling crowds blocked the city's arteries
for days, bringing chaos to commerce and
transport. Now they were restricted to the
Green — the People's Park — where they
were an obstruction to no one and their din
did not interfere with day-to-day business.

PC Stuart MacAndrews was on duty at the

Jail Square entrance to the park when the first of the brightly coloured wagons arrived. This was known as the Menagerie, the most important and profitable part of the travelling fair, and there was no doubt that they were impressive, with their yellow and red wheels and astonishing exaggerated jungle paintings in which large cats, wolves, monkeys, giraffes, elephants and camels all cohabited in scenes that paid as little attention to geographical accuracy as they did to scale.

If the living creatures contained in the cages were more subdued than their fictitious counterparts on the garish signboards, they were nevertheless still awe-inspiring. The first two wagons were each occupied by a single elephant and the third by a rhinoceros. Then came the lions, panthers and leopards, along with more unusual big cats, such as ocelots. After them, in a line that appeared to MacAndrews as though it would never end, came the zebras, onagers — from central Asia — llamas from South America, monkeys by the dozen and the most recent introduction, a gorilla from the Congo.

Bringing up the rear of the convoy were the side shows, the shooting galleries, fire-eaters, theatrical troupes, waxworks, peep shows, freak-shows and boxing booths, where bare-knuckle fighters would challenge all-comers to last a minute in the ring.

Once the entire caravan reached its allotted area inside the Green, the vehicles formed an open square. Three sides of this were composed of beast wagons, and the fourth was a sloping walkway at the top of which was a pay box and live band. The stalls and booths were erected outside the Menagerie.

But fate did not merely arrange for PC MacAndrews to witness and enjoy the gaudy wonder of it all, or thrill at the closeness of spitting, growling monsters, or even to have his eardrums assailed by the new steam-powered organs. Fate, Providence, or whatever name she was using that day, had decided that he alone should find the first body.

★ ★ ★

While Tommy Quinn and acting Detective Constable Walter Chapman, who had demonstrated an interest in photography, made a collodion plate of the jade mask in the camera room, Superintendent Henry Jarrett and Inspector Charlie Grant unwrapped and laid out the rest of the chest's contents. These were an obsidian knife, a bowl in beaten gold, large earrings in gold depicting a warrior with an eagle headdress, a gold disk on what seemed to be a neck chain, vaguely resembling mayoral regalia, and the gold turtle. Apart from the knife and earrings, all carried the same strange design that adorned the forehead of the mask.

'Bearing in mind the fact that I don't know what I am talking about,' Jarrett said, 'I just have the feeling that this is somehow incomplete.'

Charlie Grant considered the items laid out on the lost property table.

'I think I know what you mean, sir,' he agreed. 'It's an odd sort of collection, if that's what it is.'

'Difficult to see what else it can be. But of course that has nothing to do with us. Our task is to find the owner.'

'If there is an owner, why hasn't the loss been reported? Davie Black receives notification from all divisions, but nothing even remotely resembling this stuff has been reported.'

'Stolen, then? If the box was lost by thieves they would hardly be in a position to report it.'

'No, but it would be on our stolen property lists.'

Jarrett turned away from the items on the trestle and gave his attention to the now empty chest.

'The marks on the wood,' he said. 'Too random to have been a deliberate attempt at opening it.'

'Agreed, Superintendent. Accidental, I'd say.'

'Consistent with tumbling over rocks? A weir perhaps, Inspector?'

'That would be about right,' Charlie Grant admitted. 'Although it only serves to increase the possible distance it may have travelled. Donald Wylie knows his stuff when it comes to trunks, so if the planks are as tight as he says they are, and bearing in mind the amount of air in the rush matting and between the items, it might have floated and tumbled for miles before taking in enough water to cause it to sink to the bottom at Pointhouse.'

'Fair assessment,' Henry Jarrett said, 'but the question is, where did it come from? Or to be more precise, how did it get into the water, and how far did it travel before it finally sank? For all we know it could have been anywhere upriver. Rutherglen, Cambuslang and so on all the way to the hills.'

'Or it could have come down the River Kelvin,' Charlie Grant suggested. 'That river is pretty fast flowing when it is coming through the gorge, then when it meets the Clyde at Pointhouse it slows down.'

'You may be right, Inspector, but how did it get into the water in the first place? It isn't the sort of thing that could get lost overboard, and I can't imagine anyone deliberately throwing it into the river.'

'So where do we start looking?' Charlie Grant asked.

'We don't. We invite the owner to get in touch with us.'

Generally speaking, the lost property store was kept cool, but there was a Carron grate in the back wall, so Jarrett prevailed upon Sergeant Black to provide a scuttle of coal and some kindling. Before long they had a good fire going and the open chest drying off in front of it. They also draped the rush mats over the backs of chairs and wrapped the precious items in the station's supply of newly-laundered towelling. The protected artefacts they then placed in a large strawboard box which they slid beneath the shelving.

Tommy Quinn also took advantage of the blazing coals when he returned twenty or so minutes later with a full plate print squashed face down onto a sheet of glass. In no time at all the paper was crisp enough to come away from the glossy surface and withstand normal handling.

Jarrett held the photograph of the mask at arm's length.

28

'Excellent,' he said to the young Irishman. 'Where are Williamson and Russell?'

'Putting in an appearance at the Green,' Quinn replied. 'The show folk aren't a bad lot, but the fair attracts every pickpocket, robber and swindler in the district.'

'I want you to take this print to Jake McGovern at the *Advertiser*,' Jarrett continued. 'Tell him to get an engraving made of it for his front page. Say that I am inviting the owner of this piece to get in touch with us, but he or she will have to demonstrate their bona fides by providing us with a full list of the other items found in close proximity to it. And I also want all applicants to describe the type of container the objects were in. But whatever you do don't say anything to McGovern about the other artefacts, the chest or where it was found.'

'Very good, Superintendent.'

'And one other thing. Take young Chapman with you. I want you to try him out in plain clothes for a few days, and if he measures up I will see about having him transferred to the Detective Department. But for the time being he doesn't need to know anything about the find, apart from what you are going to tell McGovern.'

'Leave it to me, sir.'

'Good. And hurry back, Sergeant. I have

29

another little chore for the pair of you.'

It was at that point that Detective Constable Russell put in an unexpected appearance.

'A body has been found at the fair,' he said breathlessly. 'We think it's murder.'

'They didn't take long to get under way,' Henry Jarrett observed. 'See to it, Inspector, and keep me informed.'

'Very good, sir.' Then Charlie Grant turned to DC Russell. 'Find Dr Hamilton and accompany him to the scene. Try the mortuary beside the Sheriff Court first, and if you don't get him there he'll be in his residence in Porter Square.'

★ ★ ★

When Detective Sergeant Tommy Quinn and young Walter Chapman returned from their visit to the *Advertiser* premises, Superintendent Jarrett immediately sent them out on another less than enthralling mission, this time to trace the origin of the rush mats that had been used to wrap and protect the artefacts in the chest. For the want of a better place to start, he suggested the Botanic Gardens.

It very soon became evident that the expert on this particular subject was Abner Price, but although half a dozen of the staff recommended him without hesitation, no one knew exactly where he was. Eventually, however, they found him supervising the construction of the new glass palace.

But for Quinn's brass badge, there was little doubt that Price would have dismissed them out of hand. Even so, his manner was curt and it was quite clear that he found them something of a nuisance.

He snatched the mat from Tommy Quinn and opened it wide. It was one of the smaller ones, but just as colourful and skilfully painted.

'What do you want to know?' he demanded.

'What it is made of, where it is from and anything else you can tell us,' Tommy replied, only barely managing to keep his temper.

'Very well. It is made from the *Totora*, or *Schoeneoplectus californicus*, usually known by its common name, giant bulrush. As you can see, it is triangular in section. It is found in marshy areas in many places from western North America to South America and even on certain Pacific islands. It can be used for many purposes, from floating islands, reed boats, rafts, mats and numerous other things.'

'Anything else?'

'What else do you want?'

31

'Well, what about the painting?'

Price frowned deeply.

'I'm a botanist,' he grumbled, 'not an art expert. All I can tell you is that it is probably old, because the reed is old. Although it has recently become moist, it was cut and woven a very long time ago. The paint must have been waterproof or it would have run like ink when a letter is soaked.'

'Thank you for that, Dr Price,' Tommy Quinn said, recovering the item. 'I don't suppose you could take a guess at the nationality of the artist?'

'Wouldn't even try. It is not the thing to encroach on another's area of expertise. I suggest you ask Professor Greenaway at the university.' Price paused, then asked, 'Are you at liberty to tell me where you acquired the mat?'

'Sorry, Dr Price. That has to remain confidential for the moment.'

*   *   *

Like many of the other major attractions, the Ghost Tunnel had recently been converted to use steam power; this was a great advancement on the laborious hand-cranking device of recent times. And it was even more cleverly laid out than before. By making the train narrower and the walls closer together a fairly small room could be packed with twists and turns thus giving passengers the impression that they travelled a considerable distance.

But at that particular moment the main attraction was not the bright, inviting entrance, but the much duller, unadorned rear of the hexagonal construction and the corpse with the red patch on its chest. Much to the chagrin of Horace Dinsley, proprietor of the Ghost Tunnel and the adjacent steam-organ, Dr Hamilton insisted on the ride remaining static until he had finished his examination.

The body was in a seated position with its head slumped forward.

'Shot at extremely close range,' Dr Hamilton pointed out to Charlie Grant. 'Note the powder burns on his shirt.'

The police surgeon then placed a hand at the rear of the victim's shoulder and pressed him forward, while Charlie Grant took the weight from the front.

'No exit wound,' Hamilton muttered. 'The bullet is still in the chest cavity. Must have been a very low charge of black powder; that would also help to keep the noise down.'

'It must have happened within the last hour, Doctor,' said Inspector Grant. 'Some of the larger attractions are still being erected.'

'Agreed.' Hamilton laughed gently at this. Sudden and violent death did not have the same effect on him that it had on most people. 'Certainly within the last hour. I should say he had only just been killed when the boy found him.'

'Any sign of a struggle?'

'I'll let you know if there are other marks on the body after my preliminary examination, but that is as far as I can go, Inspector. My job is to determine the cause and time of death. You are the detective.'

Nearby, the increasingly irate Horace Dinsley was reaching boiling point.

'Every minute is costing me money,' he complained. 'We had only just assembled the show when that little brat over there found the stiff. I mean, the runt doesn't belong here. He was nosing about while we were building up a head of steam, then scurried off to tell the constable what he had found. Not one penny have I taken. Are you going to be much longer?'

Charlie Grant watched the two porters from the city mortuary dump the corpse onto an iron stretcher, then hurry it across to the blood wagon amid a sea of gawpers.

'You own this . . . whatever you call it?'

'The Ghost Tunnel,' Dinsley said. 'Yes, I am the owner, and I would like to know who is going to compensate me for loss of earnings.'

'Nobody.'

Dinsley stared at him.

'I don't think I like your manner, Sergeant.'

'It's Inspector, and I don't give a damn if you like it or not. I am advising you not to be awkward, because we have it in our power to check every nut and bolt on every contraption in this carnival for safety. You probably have a good idea how long that would take.'

'My apologies, Inspector.' Dinsley's manner softened instantly, and he became quite amiable. 'Mr Boscombe wouldn't like that at all, sir. If there is any way I can be of assistance . . . '

'You could begin by telling me the name of the victim.'

There was no hesitation in the man's reply.

'Gilbert Hayes,' Dinsley said. 'He had an archery stall out there among the hangers-on. You know the sort of thing. Loose strings and bent arrows.'

'You didn't have much of an opinion of him, then?'

'I could take him or leave him. These shows are all about having to live together, whether you like it or not. People come and go. The menagerie and the powered machines are what matter most. Everything else is just stuck on like a boil on the arse.'

Charlie could well understand that even a disparate group like this would have its hierarchy.

'Did you hear the shot?' he asked.

'Hardly. We were building up steam, the chains were clanking and the labourers were all yelling about moving something or other this way or that.'

With DCs Williamson and Russell touring the shows in the hope of finding someone who may have heard gunfire or seen the unfortunate stall-keeper in the vicinity of the Ghost Tunnel, Inspector Grant made his way to the archery booth. Grant wanted to see what could be seen from there, and perhaps find out why Gilbert Hayes was out of his territory.

The stall consisted of a dozen cheap bows and a barrel full of arrows, some straighter than others. It was just as Dinsley had said. At the point furthest away from the counter, stood three straw-filled targets that had seen better days. The concentric rings had been punctured so often that it was now almost impossible to tell them apart.

As there was nothing of interest in the archery range, Charlie moved to the next booth, where a large woman was leaning on the counter and shuffling a pack of well-worn pasteboards. Even when the inspector presented his brass badge and requested her name her expression remained impassive. It was probably the only one she had.

'Didn't know him very well,' Sadie Baker said casually, as though having a neighbour murdered was an everyday occurrence, 'Sometimes we get booths beside each other, but usually not.'

'Didn't you talk?'

'Ran out of things to say a long time ago. After you hear the stories half a dozen times that's pretty well it, isn't it? Conversation is limited to asking the bloke next door to look after your site while you're at the privy.'

'Do you know if he had a wagon?'

'One of the best. It's just round the back. A large van in red and gold with a painting of Robin Hood drawing his bow. Now, there's a laugh for you. Even Robin Hood couldn't hit the bull with that rubbish he's got. Or had, I should say.'

'Is there a wife?'

'That miserable bleeder? Wouldn't keep one.'

'But he splashed out on a new caravan?'

'His pride and joy, he called it. Mr Boscombe is very strict about the vans. Have to be painted up nice and fresh once a year, so that his is the finest train on the road.'

'Just out of interest,' Charlie asked, 'where is Boscombe's wagon?'

Sadie snorted.

'You can hardly miss it, Inspector. It's the biggest and brightest vehicle of the whole lot. One thing Cyrus N. Boscombe doesn't do is stint himself.'

Charlie made a note of this.

'To get back to Gilbert Hayes,' he said, 'haven't you a good word to say for him?'

'He was kind to his horse, so he wasn't entirely rotten.'

'Who said he was?'

'Almost everyone.'

'Including you?'

Sadie shook her head.

'I don't borrow and I don't lend,' she said. 'If you see what I mean?'

'He was a money-lender, then?'

'Ask about,' she said. 'I've said enough.'

Charlie Grant was clearly not the first to visit Gilbert Hayes' caravan since its late owner quit the place and set off on his one-way trip to oblivion. The interior was sparse and clean, yet what little there was in the way of personal possessions had been rifled and scattered as though a band of monkeys had been let loose on them. Even the crockery and utensils, of which there were just enough for the needs of a single man, were scattered and either smashed or bent on the floor. The few items of clothing that had been in the caravan's storage unit now also adorned the floor or hung from the two drawers. Nor had the searcher overlooked the single cot, which had been roughly raised from its slats and overturned. Luckily, there were no ornaments or fripperies at all, and the only book was the Holy Bible, which had been roughly flicked through and cast aside.

After a few more minutes the inspector grudgingly accepted the fact that Hayes' killer had probably found what he was looking for, although there was still a measure of doubt, so he went back outside and waited until he spotted Williamson and Russell.

'Correct me if I'm wrong,' he said to Russell, 'but you have a horsy background, haven't you?'

'Brought up with them, sir.'

'Then find out where they keep their animals and take this van back to headquarters. Tell PC Jamieson to look after the creature while the pair of you take this thing to pieces.'

'What exactly are we looking for, Inspector?' Ian Williamson asked.

'I don't think you'll find his cash,' Inspector Grant replied. 'That has almost certainly gone the way of all things, but it is also possible that the burglar was looking for a list of people who were paying through the nose for making the mistake of borrowing from this man. I think it stands to reason that whoever murdered Gilbert Hayes would probably be desperate to get his hands on a list that included his own name. On the other hand, if the prize was something else entirely, something valuable enough to kill for, I can't see Hayes just leaving it lying around for any old thief to pick up. Given a bit of luck, it might still be in there somewhere and you two are just the ferrets to find it.'

★ ★ ★

At headquarters, DC Tommy Quinn and acting DC Walter Chapman were relating to Superintendent Henry Jarrett what Dr Price had told them about the mat. They had just relayed the fact that Professor Greenaway of the University was not available when they called, but would probably be in his study tomorrow, when DC Williams and DC Russell arrived in the cobblestoned yard below; they arrived atop a many-coloured gypsy caravan, accompanied by catcalls and laughter. It was just as well that Chief Constable Rattray had decided that there was little enough to keep him interested in his office and that he would be better employed at home.

'There is really nothing more we can do about the chest and its contents until we see what kind of response we get from the *Advertiser*,' Jarrett said. 'In the meantime, you may want to see if you can give Williamson and Russell a hand, and would one of you let me know why Inspector Grant saw fit to send that contraption here.'

Since periods of no great activity were few and far between, Henry Jarrett leaned back in his chair and permitted himself the luxury of thinking about his eventual retirement plans and the very excellent Mrs Elsie Maitland; both topics being completely inseparable.

At the back of his mind there had always been the notion that he might eventually find someone and retire to a nice house with a sea view, but the demands of his profession, particularly during his years in Hong Kong, militated against such a pleasant prospect. Indeed it was not until Providence guided him back to his native land and 76 Delmont Avenue that his dreams became reality.

Four years earlier, 45-year-old corn merchant, Ernest Maitland, successfully ate himself to death and expired on Argyle Street's broad pavement. The straw that broke the camel's back was a hearty dinner at the Scotia Club. No great loss to the community at large, he at least had the common decency to leave his wife quite comfortably off.

But Elsie was not given to mourning for one day longer than etiquette demanded. After a period in full black, followed by a less austere term of grief, she turned the house into a desirable residence for single middle-class gentlemen, thereby keeping the bulk of the capital intact and living on the rents, which she preferred to call weekly tariffs. It may have been this very sensible approach to money as much as her trim figure, empha-sised by the corpulence of her late husband, which first caught the eye of Superintendent Henry Jarrett.

Mrs Maitland would have been loath to admit she hoped one of her guests might make a suitable, and perhaps better, replace-ment for the man who had literally considered her cooking good enough to die for. Not that she in any way blamed herself or her kitchen for Ernest's untimely demise. He worked and ate himself to death. She could not be faulted if he had no self-control. He was, after all, the driver of his own knife and fork.

So from the outset, Henry Jarrett and Elsie Maitland experienced a mutual attraction, although this was more implied than professed. A man of his time, Jarrett was aware of his undemonstrative nature, but the wise Mrs Maitland fully understood this and would have been shocked had he behaved in any other way. Publicly, that is. Above all other things, she prized her spotless reputation.

All in all, they understood one another and found their current arrangement eminently suitable. Without emphasizing it unduly in his plans, he had always assumed that his eventual partner, whoever she might be, would have reserves of her own to bring to the common purse, which on his marriage would by law become his property to administer as he saw fit. So without actually asking Elsie Maitland, he found himself considering whether he should keep Delmont Avenue — minus the other paying gentlemen, of course — or if it would be better to sell up and fulfil his lifelong dream of moving to the bracing, salt-laden air of the estuary, which seemed to be all the rage just then.

There was also the problem of the girls, Lizzie and Jeannie: one maid would probably be enough, and that would be cause for tears.

* * *

Half a mile away, at the southern end of the Saltmarket, Charlie Grant pushed his way through the swing doors of the city mortuary and made his way, accompanied by the sharp echoes of his boot studs, along the seemingly unending white-tiled corridor.

Dr Hamilton greeted him warmly, for he was never happier than when he was wielding the scalpel.

'Ah, just the man,' he said. 'I have something good for you.'

'The name of the killer?' Charlie asked hopefully.

'I am afraid not, Inspector.' Hamilton extended a fist which he opened to reveal a shiny lead ball. 'But you won't get a better start than this.'

Dr Hamilton then placed the bullet beneath a large magnifier. The clue was so large there was no need for a microscope.

'So it was a cap and ball pistol,' the inspector said unenthusiastically.

'A .32, to be precise. And the barrel is smoothbore, no rifling.'

'That's all very interesting, Doctor,' Charlie began, 'but — '

'It is more than interesting,' Hamilton interrupted. 'Do you see that tiny, roughly triangular mark on the ball?'

'Yes.'

'Well, that is a fault or blemish on the inside of the bullet mould. It will be on every ball cast from it. Find the owner of the mould and you almost certainly have the killer.'

'And this would stand up in court?'

'1835. One of Scotland Yard's Bow Street Runners, Henry Goddard, used bullet comparison, based on a flaw in the bullet mould, to catch a murderer and obtain a conviction. Of course, most moulds are perfectly finished, so it isn't a technique that is used very often. But where blemishes do occur, as in your case, there is precedence in law.'

'Excellent.' Charlie Grant was immensely cheered by this. Positive information had not been coming thick and fast of late. 'I don't suppose there is any indication of the type of gun used?'

'Now you are asking. To be honest, Inspector, it could have been one of those disguised firearms, a muzzle-loader, a revolver holding paper cartridges, or even some sort of homemade single-shot device. I have no way of knowing, but what I can say is that there is no rifling in the barrel and there was a very low charge of powder involved. To fire a lead ball from such close range that it burns the shirt yet lacks the power to pass through the body implies minimal gunpowder use. That would also explain why no one heard a loud bang.' Hamilton paused briefly, then went on, 'Apart from that, I don't have a great deal to add. There are no signs of violence on the body, other than the bullet wound of course.'

'The clothing?'

'His pockets appear to have been searched, perhaps for the purposes of theft. If he had a watch it is gone, along with any money he may have had on him.'

Charlie thought this over.

'That sounds like a cover for the real motive,' he said at length. 'I still favour the idea that he was killed by someone who owed him money. It wouldn't be the first time a desperate man turned on his oppressor.'

'So you think that Gilbert Hayes could have frightened his killer into taking drastic action?'

'How else can a money-lender make sure he gets paid? If he left it up to his clients' discretion he would never get it back. No, lending and enforcing go hand in hand.'

★ ★ ★

The round-faced man sitting quietly by the fire in the Clipper rose when he received a nod from the burly landlord. Almost absent-mindedly he sidled across to the bar with his empty pewter tankard to listen in on the conversation Clancy thought might interest him.

'This is Peter Rice of the *Advertiser*, gents,' the big publican told the dredger-men. 'Tell him what you were telling me and there'll be a drink in it for you.'

Billy Gregg and Gus McIvor quickly knocked back their glasses and surrendered them for refreshing, but left the talking to Captain Dan Mason.

'I don't know what you'll make of it,' Mason said honestly. 'It might be something or it might be nothing at all.'

'Try me,' Rice suggested. He had a friendly way about him that never failed to draw information out of even the most reluctant of witnesses. 'I'm sure it'll be of interest.'

Emboldened by this, Mason went on, 'To be honest, it's something we hauled up this morning. I suppose you'd call it a chest, if you know what I mean, but smaller than a seaman's trunk.'

'Aye, a good bit smaller,' Old Gus put in. 'I was thirty years at sea and we all had decent-sized trunks. Made them ourselves, usually.'

'This one had iron bands over the lid and around the body of it,' Billy Gregg said. 'Like a pirate chest.'

Peter Rice smiled.

'Have you ever seen a pirate chest?' he asked.

'No, not exactly,' Billy replied, but took no offence. 'You know what I mean. It had a foreign look about it.'

'I would say that,' Dan Mason agreed. 'Foreign is about right.'

'In what way?'

'The key-plate, I suppose. It was sort of fancy and looked ancient.'

Rice considered this.

'What was in it?' he asked, but he had a pretty good idea what they were going to say.

'They wouldn't let us see,' Mason grumbled. 'We were told we'd get a bit extra in our wages, but they wouldn't open it in front of us.'

'Who are 'they'?'

'Stainer and a few detectives.'

'I know Stainer,' Rice admitted. 'Do you know who the detectives were?'

'One of them was the Chief Constable. He told us to bugger off.'

'And the others?'

'A senior officer.'

'Jarrett?'

'I think that was the name.'

'Good lads. The others were probably Grant and Quinn.'

'A young Irish copper,' Billy volunteered.

'Good.' Peter Rice handed Clancy his tankard, but only for rinsing and hanging up on his own hook. He had had enough for the moment. What was wanted was a clear head. 'One last thing, gents. Where did you find it?'

'Pointhouse,' Mason said. 'At the mouth of the Kelvin.'

Rice rummaged deep in his pocket for what scrap he had, made sure there was no gold among it, and slapped it on the counter.

'Let the lads work their way through that, big man,' he said, and left the bar with their sincere thanks still ringing in his ears.

Now that the story of the chest was common currency he would have to get it to Mr McGovern as soon as possible, because if old Joe got it from anywhere else he would want to know why he, Peter Rice, had not come up with it and little bells would start ringing in that twisted mind. He would start wondering whether his trusted scratcher was less forthcoming than he should have been. And anyway, it was no loss as far as Rice was concerned. McGovern would see the story as being dramatic and romantic, but the full and real significance would be entirely lost on him.

Five years of chasing a myth, a legend, a piece of smoke, and now Peter Rice had found the proof he was looking for.

3

As the swirling grey smoke gradually obscured the reflection he had always disliked, and had now come to detest, the one who believed he had been condemned to this wretched place caught a glimpse of his true self and felt a rare surge of joy: The end of his suffering was near and soon he would be returning to his own time and his own land.

For now though, he still had to be on his guard against revealing his true self to the useless fools around him. They could never understand and it would only earn him mockery. Not that the opinions of these insects mattered in the least, but there was always the chance that they could in some way prevent him from carrying out his mission. After all, how could such worthless minds understand that he had two lives, a thousand years and thousands of miles apart, yet both making demands on his time and effort.

In his real world the Great Lord, King Pezelao, was dying, and there was nothing that he, the High Priest, Jaguar Claw, could do to prevent it.

Not too many days ago, but a millennium in the world of fools, the Serpent King had tested the predictive powers of the giant Pillar of Death on the Patio of Tombs and the ancient stone had foretold his death. All who were with him that day saw him embrace the monolith and had dropped to their knees when the stone rumbled and the floor shook beneath their feet. More sacrifices would soon be needed to ease the Great Lord's passage into the next world.

As the Jaguar Claw in the mirror turned away and walked silently through the gloomy Hall of Columns, flickering torches on the walls made the mosaic Sky Serpent dance. Reassuringly, the blood on the large volcanic stone altar was still fresh and the smell of death hung heavy in the impure air. Yet much more remained to be done.

He swept aside the blanket that served as a door and entered his own private room, the dwelling of the highest of all priests. No one else was permitted to enter this place unless invited to do so, for this was also the sacred initiation hall where new shamans were introduced into the darker secrets of the faith.

Although Jaguar Claw was tired and would gladly have squatted on his pallet with a blanket around his shoulders, there was far too much still to be done. Pezelao had not long to live, and it would not go well with the people if he was sent upon his long and dangerous way unprepared and unprotected. Many evil spirits lay in wait to prevent him from reaching his peace in the land of rest. If he failed in his duty as High Priest, Jaguar Claw would bring upon the people years of drought and famine.

Moreover, the king's possessions required to be purified and placed around him in the stone coffin when his time came. Golden turtles and jaguars, obsidian knives, bowls of beaten gold, and creatures of jade and pottery. The Great Lord himself would be wearing his large golden earrings depicting a warrior with an eagle headdress, his favourite Quetzal feather cloak would be around his shoulders, and the jade mask placed over his dead face. On his chest would be the gold sun disk and by his side would be ceremonial weapons of obsidian and the royal mace, a shafted stone ball engraved with the head of the Sky Serpent.

Then the smoke began to clear and his accursed face again looked back at him. Not long now, he thought, not long now. And the return could be hastened by redoubling his efforts here in this awful world. Soon he would be going home.

But first there were hearts to be harvested.

Albert Sweetman had just made a decision which precipitated the worst episode of his life. When the bow of the *Island Maid* struck the pier at Port Rannald, the passengers were given a choice of either staying put until the *White Swan* arrived in seven or eight hours, or crossing the peninsula by coach and catching the *Queen of the Heather* when she stopped briefly at Invercoll on her way to Mull. Everyone else elected to wait; Sweetman foolishly put his faith in his own judgement and set out on his great adventure, the only passenger on a dilapidated vehicle that was built for roads, but had to contend with boulders.

The enforced stoppage was a mixed blessing. Every rock on the damaged road to this miserable spot in the middle of nowhere had been pure hell. Without adequate suspension each jolt felt like a simultaneous kick in the backside and a lightning strike on the skull, and reminded him, if indeed he needed reminding, of just how much he loathed vehicular travel. Had he been gifted with even a modicum of patience he would have remained with those more tolerant people back at Port Rannald and not now be sitting by the side of the track, nursing his carpet bag and watching the rogue of a coachman clambering over the landslide that had made continued travel impossible.

'No further, sir,' the man grumbled, after deciding that the stones were too big and too many to shift. 'I'll have to turn around somehow and go back to the Port.'

Sweetman looked around him at the bleak nothingness of it all.

'Are there any people here?' he asked in a bleating manner.

'That depends on how choosy you are, and what exactly you mean.'

'What about somewhere to eat?'

'Well, there's the Dark Glen Inn if you've got a strong stomach,' the driver suggested. 'It's about half a mile on from here. The place is run by a Mrs McCreedy and her daughter.'

'That doesn't sound too bad.'

'As long as you're not superstitious you should be all right, hopefully.'

'What do you mean, 'hopefully'?'

The driver shook his head glumly.

'I'd rather say no more,' he muttered in a low voice. 'Better not push my luck in case they put the eye on me.'

'You don't seriously believe that, do you?'

'I tell you, I've said enough. Now, you can either carry on, or come back to the Port with

54

me. If you continue you've probably missed the *White Swan* by now, and if you go back the *Queen of the Heather* has no doubt been and gone. If she can stop at the pier at all, that is. Usually when there is a bump like that it takes a few days to fix it up.'

'Then I have no real choice, have I?' Sweetman stated. 'I must go on. Anyway, I'm a big lad. What have I got to fear from two women?'

'Nothing at all, I suppose.'

'And the food can't be that bad.'

'Depends on what you're used to. If you find any fur or bones just put them to one side.' The man climbed up on the board and gathered up the ribbons. 'By the way, the daughter's a starter.'

'That's good to know.'

'No problem. Get her away from her mother and give her a little silver for herself. She'll drop her drawers all right.'

Despite the obvious attraction the driver had just outlined, Albert Sweetman was of two minds and could scarcely take his eyes off the coach while the driver laboriously turned it around. Sweetman had to resist the temptation to clamber back into the vehicle and be gone from the place; even when the rattling, bumping conveyance could only just be seen amidst its own dust, he seriously considered running after it.

In the end it was a vision of Mr Hall's unsympathetic eyes, his pince-nez atop a narrow Roman nose and his tight mouth that persuaded him to see the trip through and bring back the corn. And, of course, there was the thought of a little company.

After scaling the hill of tumbledown boulders and somehow descending the other side with no mishaps, he began to pick his way cautiously along the rocky road, aware at all times of just how easy it would be to turn an ankle, or worse.

The Dark Glen Inn was around the third bend and was as forbidding as he dreaded it might be. But he had well and truly burnt his bridges, so there was nothing else for it but to see the matter through.

Suddenly, and quite understandably, he felt concern for the money belt that was buckled tightly around his ample midriff.

★   ★   ★

Albert Sweetman's predicament was the very last thing on Henry Jarrett's mind. As Inspector Grant and Sergeant Quinn waited quietly for some response, the superintendent remained hunched over a copy of the *Advertiser* brought to him a few minutes earlier by a young constable with Desk Sergeant Davie Black's compliments. At length, he straightened and, stiff-backed and devoid of expression, lifted the paper and held it up for them to see.

The engraved image was an almost perfect reproduction of Tommy Quinn's photographic print, but the headline and accompanying article left a very great deal to be desired.

CURSE OF THE SNAKE GOD

The police, at a loss to know which way to turn, have asked the Advertiser, and your editor in particular, to assist them in responding to what could be the greatest threat this city has ever faced.

It is not an exaggeration to say that a dreadful prospect hangs over each and every one of us. Somewhere out there lurks an evil beast, a thing consumed by a single wicked thought — to reclaim its hideous blue-green stone mask.

Why has it chosen our fair city as the battlefield between good and evil? Well, it just so happens that the Advertiser is in a position to answer that. Although the police attempted to conceal this fact, we have learned that a strange and accursed chest has been dredged up from the mud and ooze of the Clyde. Like Pandora's Box its opening has unleashed wickedness and the seeds of our destruction.

On a more prosaic level, if you know anything about this dreadful object please report to the City of Glasgow Police, providing them with a full inventory of the contents of the chest and any other details you may feel are relevant.

In the meantime, copies of Professor Whiteside's excellent pamphlet, PRO-TECTING YOURSELF AND YOUR FAMILY FROM PRIMITIVE EVIL, can be had from the Advertiser office for threepence each.

[Jake McGovern, Editor & Prop.]

'I didn't say any of those things to him,' Tommy Quinn offered, a touch of panic in his voice.

'Of course you didn't.' Jarrett folded the paper and consigned it to his waste basket. 'The man is a bigger menace than his mythical demon.'

But Charlie Grant wasn't so sure.

'McGovern has certainly cut down the number of opportunists and other chancers who would otherwise be swarming over Davie

Black's desk in the hope of striking it lucky.'

'You are not suggesting that we turn him into some sort of public-spirited citizen, Inspector?'

'No, of course not, sir. He's an opportunist of the worst kind, but he might just keep the streets free of rogues and drunks after dark for a few nights.'

'The proverbial silver lining? I dare say that might be one result, even if he didn't intend it that way.' Jarrett paused briefly, then, 'Right, now you have a more pressing matter in hand. Sergeant Quinn and young Chapman can continue to investigate this unusual piece of lost property, but your Glasgow Green murder case is much more important. I don't have to point out that this is not a gun city, Inspector. Crimes involving firearms are few and far between, and I would like to keep it that way. It is essential that you haul this character out of circulation and into the lock-up just as soon as possible.'

Charlie Grant nodded his agreement.

'If Williamson and Russell unearth anything of interest in the caravan it could point to the killer, the motive or both,' he said. 'In the meantime I have to talk to one member of the showground community who knows more about guns than any of the others.'

Just then, Ian Williamson arrived, a

self-satisfied grin on his face and a metal money-box in his hands.

'One of the floorboards had fake nail heads,' he said happily. 'Not the sort of thing your amateur burglar would have thought to look for.'

'Great work, Constable,' Charlie Grant said, taking possession of the item. 'You missed your true calling.'

'Still plenty of time for that, sir. I'll see how my career develops.'

The tiny silver key was still in its lock. The inspector placed the box on Jarrett's desk, unlocked it and lifted the lid. Inside was a bundle of paper money, a small Stamford cash-book, with a green cloth cover and red tape spine, and another small key.

'Just over the hundred,' Charlie announced after flicking through the notes. 'Tidy little sum.'

Henry Jarrett lifted the cash-book and turned the first few pages over.

'A set of initials for each page with a record of payments made. He had six of them by the throat, each parting with two pounds every Saturday.'

'Twelve pounds a week?' Tommy Quinn whistled gently. 'That's more than the Chief Constable earns.'

'And a bloody sight more than he's worth,' Charlie put in before he could stop himself.

'Inspector,' Superintendent Jarrett said firmly, 'enough, if you don't mind.'

'Apologies, sir.' The inspector tapped the tin box. 'What is the correct procedure regarding ill-gotten gains?'

'Frankly, I have no idea. If this money has been acquired through illegal money-lending, I suppose it is up to the Sheriff Court to decide what to do with it. For the time being, I think you should lodge it in Sergeant Black's lost property room, along with the other items.'

'And the caravan?'

'That is more of a problem. One thing I do know, the Chief Constable is going to be less than delighted when he comes in tomorrow morning and sees that thing in the yard.'

'If I might make a suggestion,' DC Russell offered, 'we could return it to the fairground and keep a watch on it, just in case the thief tries again.'

'Wouldn't work.' Charlie Grant lifted the Stamford cash-book. 'As soon as I start asking for names to go with these initials everyone will know we found whatever there was to find.'

'Sorry, Inspector.'

'Don't mention it, Constable. You contributed and that gets remembered.' Grant fished out his notebook and copied the initials into it, then returned the cash-book to the box with the money. 'What about the other key, Superintendent?'

'Almost certainly a safe-deposit box,' Jarrett said, 'but where is it? According to their poster, the menagerie and side-shows cover the whole country from Penzance to Inverness. The only thing on the key is a number, so the box it opens could be any town, anywhere. Frankly, Inspector, I don't think we'll ever know.'

'I agree absolutely, sir,' Charlie said, adding, 'Is there any sense in proceeding with the enquiries today? The place will be milling like a cattle auction.'

'No, wait until tomorrow morning. But for God's sake think up something to do with the van.'

'It's a bit eye-catching,' Tommy Quinn said. 'If PC Jamieson could get it into the stable block and throw a tarp over it I don't think there would be any problem. I don't recall the CC ever going down there.'

And that, as far as all were concerned, was the perfect answer.

★ ★ ★

A long time ago, Johannes Kirchner had left German East Africa in pursuit of riches. It had never been his intention to climb the ladder, or found a business empire of his own. What Kirchner wanted was to find a fortune that was ready-made and waiting for the right man. He was a treasure-hunter and he had lived in almost every country where legends are born.

He had sought them all: Eldorado in the jungles of South America, the Gates to Atlantis in the Azorean highlands, Shambhala in Tibet and the Lost City of the Monkey God in the Yucatan. At different times he had hunted with or fought against others of his own kind. For the last five months, though, he had been a paying guest of Mrs Hyslop at 94 Benton Mews, near the Great Western Road, having been drawn across the Atlantic from Belize by what had become known among the brethren of searchers as the Hamilton Question.

All doubts he may have harboured about the wisdom of moving to this foreign city had just disappeared as he braced himself on his knuckles and stared unblinkingly at the newspaper he had spread out on the table. The idiotic headline was of no importance whatsoever and the article itself was sensational drivel, but the large etched picture in the middle of the page required no caption. Nor could it be given one by the idiot who

63

wrote the piece for that individual had not the first idea of what he was dealing with. But Kirchner knew all about the jade mask. He knew beyond a shadow of a doubt that it was the death mask of an ancient king, Pezelao, who had devoted his entire life to adoring and appeasing Cocijo — God of rain, Cozobi — God of corn, Pecala — God of dreams and excess, and, most feared of all, Copijcha, the snake-tongued God of the sun and war.

One thing was sure, Kirchner wasn't the only one intrigued by the Hamilton Question. Some else had arrived at about the same time as himself and was asking the right questions in the right places.

★ ★ ★

Elisha Bradwell was originally a native of Richmond, Virginia, but now considered himself to be a citizen of the world. Had it not been for the lure of treasure he would have been as patriotic as the next man, and perhaps by now would have eagerly volunteered to become another corpse among many on some churned and bloody battlefield. As it was, another dead hero more or less wouldn't make a pick of difference to the whole stupid madness of it all.

When the initial shock of seeing the jade

mask on the front of the local rag finally wore off, Bradwell strode across to the glazed doors, drew them open and stepped out onto the balcony of his apartment at the Victoria Hotel, where his Galilean binoculars lay on a small table, awaiting further use. Day after day, from when he first descended the gangplank of the *Mistress of the Atlantic*, and somehow managed to cope with the rigours of dry land for the first time since leaving Buenos Aires, he had watched patiently those who visited the Architectural Records office until he finally saw a face from the past; it was that of a man he had worked with on more than one occasion. They had hunted for the Poverty Island gold in Lake Michigan, and the Great Treasure of Lima, reputedly buried on Cocos Island by the Portuguese pirate, Benita Bonito, but neither expedition had been successful. Nevertheless, both men had sufficient luck with smaller searches to be able to continue to fund the big ones.

The presence of the East African, Johannes Kirchner, represented the seal of approval Bradwell was hoping for; Kirchner had a nose for the real thing, and had expressed considerable interest in the Hamilton Question the last time they met in Havana. He had also made it clear that he wasn't going to share this one. Both men had known about the legend of the *Nuestra Senora de Cartagena* long before Hamilton's piece was published in the *New York Science Review*, but had assumed on balance that it was probably apocryphal. Now the legend had been proved, the treasure was available to whoever found it and not for splitting down the middle.

⋆　⋆　⋆

It was with considerable trepidation that Albert Sweetman sat down at the rough-hewn table in the Dark Glen Inn and waited for his meal. But it was not the food that really concerned him. He was still recovering from the tongue-lashing he had received from the terrifying Mrs McCreedy, who had a very low opinion of men in general and salesmen in particular. Worst of all to her mind, he was a Lowlander and, therefore, as untrustworthy as they come. After demanding payment in advance for food and accommodation, she had told him to go and sit in that place until she found him something to eat.

At least there was a roaring fire, even if it did burn dried cow chips. Coal, he was told, was too expensive for the local carter to bring this far and wood was a scarcity on such rocky hillsides, where hairy, ill-kempt cattle grazed on the thin grass and devoured any sapling that was brave enough to take root.

Eventually, for there was no clock in evidence and no obvious reason for Mrs McCreedy and her daughter, Eileen, to pay any attention to the passing of time, the girl arrived with a tray on which was a large pewter plate piled high with potatoes and a dark, stringy meat. Sweetman hoped it was beef, but was afraid to ask.

At least it came with a flagon of ale.

'We brew it ourselves,' the girl said without being asked. She was much warmer than her mother and seemed even quite eager to talk. The coachman, it seemed, had not exaggerated. 'It's very powerful.'

'Good.' He tried it and found it quite acceptable. But something else was on his mind. 'I'm told you like a bit of silver.'

The girl's expression hardened.

'Who told you about that?' she whispered hoarsely.

'The coach driver.'

'Well . . . perhaps, but he had no right to talk that way. It sounds worse than it is. The truth is, I'm saving up in the hope of getting married someday. I don't have a father to put up a dowry.'

'What would you say to half a crown?'

Her eyes widened.

'Are you a rich man?' she breathed.

'Fairly,' Sweetman admitted. 'In fact, quite considerably.'

'In that case, we'll talk about it in your room. But for now you'd better eat up so that she doesn't suspect anything. She watches me like a hawk, you know.'

Immensely buoyed up by this upturn in his fortunes, Sweetman proceeded to do justice to the meal and found it better by far than he expected.

Eventually, and quite bounding with anticipation, he followed Eileen McCreedy up the narrow winding stairs to an equally narrow passage, strongly reminiscent of one of the lesser steamboats. Even the room he was shown to was little more than a cabin, with a single bunk and one tiny window, the latter evidence of the effect of Window Tax.

'You should be warm enough here, sir,' the girl said, louder than required so that anyone listening down in the hallway would assume that all was above board and formal. 'I'll find you another blanket.'

Sweetman dug into his waistcoat pocket and produced a shiny half-crown, which he pressed into her hand.

'You'll do instead,' he said softly. 'I don't believe in long introductions.'

'I don't know.' She looked concerned and

for a moment the hefty salesman thought he had made a capital blunder. But his judgement had not failed him. 'I mean I don't know where she is.'

Albert Sweetman put a finger to his lips and listened carefully for a sound, any sound. After a few moments there came from far away the unmistakable clattering of metal plates and utensils.

'There you are,' he whispered. 'As happy as a pig in shit.'

He lifted the giggling girl and dumped her onto the bed. She was still clutching her precious half-crown against her chest.

'Have you more of these?' she asked quietly.

'No end of them.' Sweetman chuckled and shoved her plain dress up around her middle. 'But first we'll have your drawers away.'

It was at such moments, and in a wide variety of rooms in a hundred towns that Albert Sweetman was most at home. This was what he was born for and what he would cheerfully die for. In such a state of blessed oblivion, when time ceases to pass and the only sounds are those made by the participants, menace can glide in unexpected and unobserved.

With the touch of cold metal on the skin of his backside, followed immediately by the sharp click of the hammer of a percussion fowling piece, came the rising of perspiration on Sweetman's forehead.

'Get to your feet, you vile creature,' Mrs McCreedy hissed angrily, 'or I'll blow a new arse in you.'

The sudden shock having put an immediate end to his favourite sport, Sweetman rolled off the narrow bed and dragged up his turkey red cotton johns, but in his nervous state he could not make the mother-of-pearl buttons and tight little buttonholes engage properly.

'I don't understand,' he pleaded, unable to take his eyes off the muzzle of the old gun. 'What have I done?'

'Be quiet!' Mrs McCreedy raised the weapon until it was pointing at his face. 'You come here, boasting about your wealth and thinking you can exercise your privilege to ravish young maidens at will.'

The burly salesman was both horrified and terrified.

'Madam is joshing,' he blurted. 'I have never ravished anyone in my life, and as far as being a maiden is concerned, she has had more in the saddle than a seaside donkey.'

'Are you trying to make me kill you?' the woman demanded, advancing upon him until she could prod his stomach with the gun's muzzle. This she did repeatedly until he had backed to the wall and had nowhere left to go. 'You'd never be found, so you'd better think of doing the right thing.'

'What right thing?'

'You ruined her. You must marry her.'

'This must be a bloody nightmare,' Sweetman complained, but respectfully. 'If anyone is getting ruined it's me.'

'You could do worse.' Mrs McCreedy jerked her head in the direction of the girl, who was still protecting her prize in a tight fist. 'You have a choice, fat one. Either I send for Reverend Gillen or Sergeant Clarke. Make an honest woman of her, or be escorted to Fort William to face a charge of ravishing. The circuit judge gets there about three times a year, so you'll have plenty of time to find a good lawyer.'

Albert Sweetman shook his head until it was in danger of coming loose.

'This is nothing but a trick,' he objected miserably. 'You want me to offer you money, don't you? Just how many poor strangers have the pair of you bled?'

Mrs McCreedy pressed the metal tube into his belly, but this time did not withdraw it.

'Insulting a simple girl won't help you,' she said. 'You'll stay right here under lock and key until you decide to do the right thing, or until I decide to fetch Sergeant Clarke.'

Then the door slammed shut, a key rattled in its lock and Albert Sweetman found himself entirely alone and utterly helpless. How could he ever explain his predicament to Mr Hall? Not that it would come as a shock to the old bugger, of course. In fact, a clause had been added to their partnership agreement to the extent that if either brought the firm into disrepute he would forfeit his shares to the other. So his own forty-nine per cent would join Mr Hall's fifty-one per cent in the twinkling of an eye. In short, Mr Hall would not be exactly heartbroken if Albert Sweetman wound up in the clink, or, better yet, was hanged.

And what would Mrs Maitland think of him? Then he remembered the unfortunate incident when he first arrived at 76 Delmont Avenue and assumed wrongly that the lady would think it funny or raunchy to have a chuckling, overweight salesman hoist her linen and grab her drawers. Since that awful day, when he came within a gnat's whisker of being chucked down the front steps, he had been as good as gold. But Mrs Maitland probably subscribed to the belief that a leopard does not change its spots, nor a salesman his coarse jokes, so it might not be a good idea to rely on any character reference she might choose to pen. A good lady, certainly, but one with a long memory.

And then there was Superintendent Henry Jarrett. Albert Sweetman shuddered at the thought of asking that man for help. He had made it perfectly clear on a number of occasions that he had little time for idle chatter and frivolity, which, it had to be admitted, were the successful salesman's stock in trade. And there was little or no doubt in Sweetman's mind that there was more between Mrs Maitland and Jarrett than the relationship of landlady and lodger. Yet it could never be confirmed. Even during his brief involvement with the maid, Jeannie, Sweetman was none the wiser, because it soon became obvious that the girls were just as much in the dark as he was, and that no amount of listening at the wall with a tumbler or peeking through keyholes had added one whit to their fund of knowledge.

All in all, then, it was a grim situation, out of which Sweetman could see no clear road. Until something presented itself the best he could hope for was that they continued to feed him.

* * *

Henry Jarrett, for his part, enjoyed an excellent meal of green pea soup, braised ham and vegetables, followed by blancmange, before retiring to his room to relax in front of his Wardian fern case, a million miles from headquarters and the events of the day.

But his tranquillity was not destined to last. There was a gentle rap on the door and Elsie Maitland entered. She closed it behind her and glided to his side. Then she placed a hand on his shoulder to prevent him from rising, because she had something to say and did not want the distraction of following him as he strode around the room in his usual, off-putting manner.

'Tell me exactly what was going on in the dining room this evening,' she said softly. 'The atmosphere was almost as thick as the pea soup. Mr Stainer and you were quite obviously not talking and poor Mr McConnell didn't know where to put himself. I am only thankful that Mr Sweetman is off on his business trip, because he would almost certainly have had something to say.'

Jarrett stuck his thumbs in his waistcoat pockets and made it quite clear that he would not be brow-beaten.

'If you had been in the room when I arrived,' he stated, 'you would have noticed that I acknowledged Mr Stainer, but received no response whatsoever. Mr McConnell, who sees everything and says nothing, was visibly embarrassed by the incident, while I was determined not to be cut a second time.'

'There must have been a reason for it, surely?'

'Oh, there was a reason alright. Circumstance decreed that Mr Stainer and I should find ourselves locking horns over a legal matter.'

Elsie Maitland was shocked.

'He has fallen foul of the law?' she breathed.

'That is not what I said. From time to time the police become embroiled in what ought to be civil affairs. Mr Stainer and I have disagreed over what should be done with certain items of lost property. He was to submit a claim to the Crown for its estimated value, while I am obliged to at least make an attempt to find the true owner. To further complicate things, Chief Constable Rattray has taken it upon himself to side with the Clyde Navigation Trust.'

'Oh, that is awkward,' Elsie Maitland said, without going as far as admitting she had perhaps been a bit hasty. 'Does it concern that horrible thing on the cover of the *Advertiser*?'

Henry Jarrett stared at her in horror.

'You haven't started to take that scurrilous rag, have you?' he demanded.

'Most certainly not!' Mrs Maitland was offended and showed it. 'I caught the girls scaring each other with it, though how they got their hands on it I shudder to think. I'll have it out with them afterwards and make sure it doesn't happen again.'

★ ★ ★

Perhaps Johannes Kirchner ought to have been surprised when Mrs Hyslop arrived at his door late in the evening with a sealed letter she had found on the doormat at 94 Benton Mews, but after the best part of three decades searching every corner of the globe for treasure, mysterious messages at odd hours scarcely caused him to raise an eyebrow.

He burst open the red wax disk with his thumbnail and shook open the treble-folded sheets. It was brief, to the point and unsigned. The note conveyed an offer to supply Kirchner with information Dr Hamilton had not included in the *New York Science Review* article in exchange for one thousand pounds in cash. The rendezvous spot was the foyer of Graham's Music Hall in the Trongate, at nine o'clock that evening.

Kirchner unbuckled his valise, brought out the .38 pistol and, letting it slide into his coat pocket, left the room, descending quickly to the hallway. After notifying Mrs Hyslop that he was going out and might not be back for some hours, he stepped out into the cool night and proceeded swiftly along Benton Mews to the Great Western Road where he was more or less guaranteed a Hansom cab within a minute or so.

4

DS Tommy Quinn, with Acting DC Walter Chapman in tow, was obliged to make his own way to the university because DI Grant with DCs Williamson and Russell had commandeered the Department's sole wagonette to resume their enquiries at the fair on Glasgow Green. However, PC Jamieson was instructed by Henry Jarrett to return immediately to headquarters, just in case the vehicle was required.

In fact, Superintendent Jarrett was at his office window when Domino trotted into the yard and Jamieson drew the Vanner and wagonette to a halt and stepped down onto the cobbles.

Just then, the chief's light reverie was interrupted by a knock on the door and the appearance of a young constable.

'Excuse, sir,' the boy said, 'but Sergeant Black wishes to inform you that there is a gent in the foyer who is demanding to talk to you.'

'Any idea what he wants?' Jarrett asked.

'Sorry, sir. He will only talk to our superior.'

'Will he indeed.' Jarrett returned to his desk and took his rightful place in the large leather chair. 'Then you had better show him in, lad. Can't keep the gent waiting.'

The new arrival was a tall, cadaverous individual, who seemed to be dressed more for the evening than the forenoon. When Jarrett invited him to sit he did so, then produced a silver card case and offered a carte-de-visite, which the superintendent accepted and studied briefly. 'Gideon Mallam, Guatemalan Consul, 22 Royal Exchange Square.' Since it was clearly an expensive piece of work, he returned it to his visitor who put it back in the case without a word.

'Guatemalan Consul,' Jarrett said for the sake of saying something.

'Yes. No doubt you probably imagined someone in my line of work would be of Hispanic origins.'

'To be frank, Mr Mallam, I didn't really imagine anything. We don't get many consular visits here. Perhaps visitors from the New World are better behaved than most.'

Mallam smiled wanly.

'I am not here because a Guatemalan has been detained in one of your cells, Superintendent.'

'Then why are you here?'

Mallam reached into his coat pocket and

withdrew a large folded newspaper cutting. Even before the man opened it Jarrett knew exactly what it was.

'The mask,' Mallam said coldly. 'I would like it returned, please.'

'It belongs to you?'

'It belongs to the sovereign state of Guatemala.'

'Can you prove this?'

'There is no need for me to prove it. The piece is obviously part of a tomb robber's hoard.'

'It may very well be,' Jarrett admitted, 'but it is not obviously so. There are any number of explanations for its presence here.'

'Quite, but ultimately it was stolen from a Guatemalan tomb.'

'Why Guatemalan?'

Gideon Mallam tapped the picture.

'It states clearly that the jade is blue green,' he said. 'That is the highest quality. It comes from Guatemala.'

'Initially, I dare say, but that does not prove that the workmanship is Guatemalan.'

'With respect, Superintendent. Do you know anything about jade?'

'I served with the Hong Kong police,' Jarrett replied. 'Believe me, Mr Mallam, you won't teach the Chinese anything about jade.'

Mallam took a deep breath.

'The article, ridiculously sensational though it may be, might turn out to be more prophetic than you realize. Put another way, the mask could bring with it a dreadful curse, though perhaps not of the supernatural variety.'

'I fail to understand, Mr Mallam,' Jarrett admitted.

'Let us hope you never have cause to.' Gideon Mallam rose and put on his hat in preparation for taking his leave. 'Meanwhile, Superintendent, I intend to place a formal request with your superiors for the return of the mask and any other items you are holding.'

Henry Jarrett also got to his feet and crossed to the door, which he drew open for the gentleman.

'Please do, Mr Mallam,' he said, and noting the frown of confusion on the other's face, Jarrett explained. 'You would make my task very much easier if you would.'

Mallam had no sooner departed than the young constable was back.

'Sorry, sir,' he said cautiously, 'but the Chief Constable requests your presence in his office immediately.'

This, of course, came as no surprise to Superintendent Jarrett, who had been expecting a summons from above ever since he arrived at headquarters that morning. The CC was never one to forgive and forget, preferring instead to mull over every slight, real or imagined, until the point was reached where it had to be resolved.

On this occasion, Rattray scarcely allowed Henry Jarrett to close the office door before starting on him.

'You made a bloody fool of me!' he stated loudly. 'I gave you a direct order and you went out of your way to humiliate me in front of representatives of the Clyde Navigation Trust.'

But the superintendent had anticipated no less than this and had his answer ready.

'You put me in an awkward position, sir,' he said truthfully. 'Compliance was not possible.'

'Compliance is always possible, Jarrett. All you have to do is obey the order.'

'There is the question of actual ownership, sir.'

'Yes, but that is for the court to decide. Your duty is merely to carry out my orders and hand over the goods.'

'To whom, Chief Constable?'

'To the Queen's and Lord Treasurer's Remembrancer in Edinburgh, of course. Or have you taken it upon yourself to make decisions for the Crown?'

'Certainly not, sir,' Jarrett replied, 'but I'm afraid it isn't that simple. Another claim — '

'There isn't another claim, Jarrett, so comply with my instructions and do it now.'

'If you will permit me to finish, sir. You will shortly be receiving an official request from the representative of the Guatemalan government for the return of what they say are plundered grave goods. That, I think, will muddy the waters.'

Rattray blinked and his lips moved, but for several moments nothing intelligible emerged from them. Then he once more found his voice.

'What representatives?' he asked, but now less forcibly.

'Gideon Mallam, Consul for Guatemala. Their official office is as 22 Royal Exchange Square.'

The CC clasped his hands on his belly and twiddled his thumbs vigorously as he sought a suitable reply.

'I am not convinced that there is a problem, Jarrett,' he said at length. 'Virtually every object in the British Museum has been acquired by the time-honoured process of lifting and taking away. All suggestions that such objects should be returned to their so-called rightful owners fall upon deaf ears.'

'Indeed so, sir,' Jarrett agreed, 'but we

could avoid a dispute with the Crown and a diplomatic quarrel by simply letting both parties know that the box and its contents are being treated as circumstantial evidence in a murder investigation, and that the items will be released as soon as said investigation is completed.'

'Is that true? Are we holding on to the artefacts because they relate to a murder enquiry?'

'There is a murder,' the superintendent admitted, 'and we are holding on to the objects.'

Rattray considered him quizzically.

'I am not absolutely sure that you just answered my questions, Jarrett,' he said.

'Let me put it this way, sir,' Henry Jarrett replied, 'if you were unavailable for a period I would be perfectly justified in telling the claimants that I am not in a position to release any information or make any final decisions.'

Chief Constable Rattray rose from his throne and absent-mindedly reached for his coat. Still, preoccupied with the possible implications of this course, he plonked his hat on his head and plucked his silver-topped cane from the elephant's foot stand.

'I believe I feel a recurrence of my old complaint, Jarrett,' he said firmly. 'Rest is the only thing for it. I'll be back in three or four days and then I am going to make a decision. Now, where's my bloody chariot?'

★ ★ ★

Nigel Greenaway's relaxed and cheery manner came as a welcome surprise to Tommy Quinn, who had anticipated a repeat of his less than pleasant encounter with Price at the Botanic Gardens.

At the professor's insistence DS Quinn took a high-backed cane chair, but Acting DC Chapman thought it more appropriate to remain standing.

For quite some time Greenaway hunched over the painted mat.

'Interesting,' he said after completing his first examination of the item. 'But you do realize that this has nothing to do with the mask, don't you?'

'Actually, no, Professor,' Quinn admitted. 'We assumed that they were somehow connected.'

'Understandable, but in fact the mat is from the Lake Titicaca region of Bolivia. The jade mask is possibly Zapotec from Oaxaca.'

'And the mats?'

'Mere wrappings. They could have been used many times by the Spaniards for just that purpose, just as you might wrap an object in a cotton tea towel to protect it on its travels. It would be whatever came to hand.'

Now that the mat was no longer of interest, Tommy Quinn returned it to his leather case and instead produced an original full-plate photograph of the jade mask.

'I thought you would prefer to see a photograph of the original object, Professor,' he said, 'rather than the engraving.'

'Indeed I would,' Greenaway took the print and nodded happily as he studied it. 'No doubt you wish me to tell you all about it?'

'I would be much obliged, Professor.'

'Then let us see what we can do, although you must appreciate that much of it is myth or legend.'

'There is a difference?'

'A myth is an entirely fictitious explanation for a given phenomenon, while a legend very often has some basis in fact, however small.' Greenaway made himself comfortable and launched into a story which he had obviously related many times. 'What we have here, gentlemen, is a combination of two legends, the first concerning a great treasure ship and the second an attempt at financing the rebellion of Charles Edward Stuart.

'In the beginning, the Conquistadores would melt down any gold or silver artefact and recast the precious metals as roughly-shaped ingots, which were then transported to Spain. In the course of time, the weird and wonderful objects being located by the Spaniards in the New World came to have a far greater value to wealthy Europeans than their raw bullion worth. A figurine, say, weighing sixteen ounces, might have a bullion value of twenty or thirty pounds, but as a desirable piece of art the same item could sell at auction for hundreds, or even thousands of pounds. It made sense, then, that the Spanish king, wishing to support the Jacobite rebellion of 1745, would send something that would raise a vast fortune considerably in excess of a few chests full of coins or bullion. And there was the added benefit of relative lightness. Trunks full of gold would be difficult to move, whereas objects and works of art could be easily lifted and transported by a small number of men.

'Having said that, the Spaniards had their own problems. During certain periods, such as the War of Spanish Succession, it was considered unsafe for the gold ship to be on the high seas, so great treasure houses were built in various places, including Hispaniola, which is now Cuba.

'According to this legend, it was from one of these treasure houses that a Spanish vessel,

Nuestra Señora de Cartagena, set sail for Spain in 1745. But on that particular voyage the captain was instructed to make for a bay on the west coast of Scotland, where he was to offload an extremely valuable consignment. It was the entire contents of the tomb of a Zapotec king, divided between eight identical chests.

'Now, local legend has it that a group of Jacobites were instructed to receive a magnificent gift from the king of Spain and to convey it to a place of safety. But before the Spaniards arrived the Jacobites were ambushed and slaughtered by a group of assassins in the pay of a traitor. However, one of the injured men who survived by pretending to be dead, counted eight treasure chests being carried up the beach and loaded onto a wagon. After that, there is only silence.'

Although normally quite imperturbable, Tommy Quinn reflected surprise.

'Eight?'

'Exactly,' Professor Greenaway said. 'May I ask how many boxes you have recovered?'

DS Quinn glanced at young Walter Chapman who was still enthusiastically scribbling every dot and comma into his notebook. It was tempting to call a halt to the boy's over-zealous activities, just in case

Superintendent Jarrett took exception to any of the entries, but somehow that did not seem to be the right and proper introduction to procedure.

'One,' he said apologetically.

Greenaway frowned deeply.

'How very surprising. Frankly, Sergeant, that doesn't make sense. Unless, of course, the other seven chests are also at the bottom of the river.'

'We don't think so, Professor. Although we didn't know the total number until now, we assumed that there might be others.' As he prepared to take his leave, Tommy Quinn could hardly help wondering what Superintendent Jarrett was going to make of this fresh information. 'Well, I must thank you for all your help, Professor. If you do hear of anything that might assist us, please drop me a line. I would be most grateful.'

★ ★ ★

In the kitchen at 76 Delmont Avenue, Lizzie Gill, one of Mrs Maitland's two maids-of-all-work, was scrubbing the terracotta tiles immediately in front of the large Flavel cooker. She was unexpectedly joined by her counterpart, Jeannie Craig. Unexpectedly, that is, because the lady of the house had left them detailed instructions before departing for town and expected them to be carried out to the letter.

'What are you doing down here?' Lizzie asked, sitting back on her heels. 'You can't have done the men's rooms yet. If Mrs Maitland — '

'Oh, don't worry about that. She's off to Wylie and Lochhead's for some new bedding, so we won't have her on our necks before midday.' Jeannie waved a letter at her. 'Anyway, this is more important.'

'Where did you get that? If she finds out you've been rummaging in the rooms you'll get what not. You should keep your hands off things that don't concern you.'

'But this does concern me. And it concerns you too, Miss Gill. It was on Jarrett's mantelpiece. He must have put it there last night because it wasn't there yesterday.' Jeannie shook the folds out of the paper. 'It was sent to police headquarters. Do you want to know what it says?'

Lizzie dumped the scrubbing brush in the bucket and wiped her hands on the already damp apron.

'Oh, all right,' she said, a little disappointed with herself at having yielded to normal curiosity when she liked to pretend that she was above such things. 'Then you'd better get it put back where it belongs. She would be particularly angry if it was the superintendent's private property.'

'Yes, and we all know why, don't we?'

'I really don't know what you mean.'

'Come off your high horse. You love to make out that you don't understand earthly matters, but when it comes down to it you're no better than those you talk about.' Jeannie made a face at her. 'When me and old Sweetman were on speaking terms he told me about you and your photographer, the one Jarrett threw out of the house.'

'He had no right to talk about me,' Lizzie said angrily. 'Anyway, it was Mrs Maitland who showed him the door, not Superintendent Jarrett. It isn't his house to order people in and out of.'

'Not yet, perhaps, but things are about to change. They might not be married, but they're almost as good as.'

'Rubbish.'

'Not rubbish. Sweetman says he punches her ticket.'

'Well, you should be more picky when it comes to what you believe, my girl. What Sweetman doesn't know he makes up.'

'He didn't make it up. Do you want to hear it or not?'

'Might as well.'

'Right, then listen to what has been going on behind our backs, then you can tell me if you are still loyal to the pair of them.'

'*Superintendent Henry Jarrett,*' Jeannie began, 'etcetera and so forth,

'*Dear Sir,*

'*It is with great pleasure that I forward full details of the property at Shore Road, Largs.*

'*It is in effect an elegant detached villa, built as a summer home during the first decade of this century. It is built entirely of red sandstone on two floors, with an additional eighty square yards of loft space which may, of course, be developed.*'

There were three sheets in all, and Lizzie Gill listened quietly while Jeannie read out a description of each of the rooms and the main features of the grounds on which the house sat. Finally, and with great emphasis, the girl reached the most important part.

'*The present owners keep one servant girl and this has proved to be perfectly adequate for their needs.*

'*J. Wilson Pettigrew,*

'*House Factor.*'

Jeannie stared long at Lizzie, but there was still no response from that quarter. Finally Lizzie said, 'But that's their business. It has nothing to do with us.'

'Of course it has. It says 'one servant'. If

they don't have paying guests they won't need both of us, will they?'

'No, I suppose not.'

Jeannie folded the letter and pushed it back inside the envelope.

'The trouble with you, Lizzie Gill,' she said sharply, 'is that you're too accepting. You're quite prepared to let them kick you around without making any attempt to stand up for yourself.'

'What else can we do? Mrs Maitland pays our wages, so if she decides she can get by with one skivvy instead of two maids then that's that.'

'Well, that may be that as far as you're concerned, but speaking personally I'm not taking it lying down. From now on I'm going to do everything I can to let her see that she can't do without me. If anyone is going to be shown the door, Miss, it'll be you, not me.'

★   ★   ★

While Williamson and Russell toured the stalls hopeful of more information on the final comings and goings of the late Gilbert Hayes, Inspector Grant visited the booth of the one man in the fairground who was most likely to know about the type of weapon used in the murder.

Wesley Bain had expected a visit from the law ever since the body had been found. What surprised him was the fact that no uniform or plain-clothes officer had come anywhere near him on the previous day. But now this oversight was being rectified. He watched Charlie Grant sauntering casually in his direction and wondered just who he thought he was fooling.

Inspector Grant lifted a rifle and tested the chain that kept it firmly tied to the counter.

'Can't be turned on the mob,' Bain offered without being asked. 'Strictly for the target.'

Charlie Grant allowed the showman to insert a paper cartridge and percussion cap into the breech, then put the butt to his shoulder and drew a bead on the tin duck. To hit it the ball had first to pass through a hole in a sheet of metal, and this it did with remarkable ease. The duck fell backwards, dead for the thousandth time.

'Excellent shot,' Bain said happily.

Charlie laid the rifle on the well worn bench.

'I didn't think you would give a copper anything less than a full charge of black powder and a corrected front sight,' he offered. 'I saw you adjust it with your thumb.'

The man grinned sheepishly.

'You know how it goes,' he said, glancing at

the brass badge in the inspector's open palm. 'Have to make a living, you know. If everybody won a prize I would be out of business by dinner time, and the same would apply if no one did. It's all a question of striking a happy medium.'

'I dare say, but I'm not really interested in your little fiddles right now.' Charlie lifted the wooden flap and joined Bain in the booth. 'Let me see your bullet mould.'

Wesley Bain frowned, but obliged immediately by fetching the tool from a drawer, flipping it over and presenting Inspector Grant with the handles. At first glance the mould looked like a pair of pliers with the addition of a third, smaller handle at the business end.

'The bore?' Charlie asked.

'.22.'

'Any others?'

'No, that's the only one.'

Charlie twisted the little handle sideways and opened the jaws of the tool. He then examined the polished inside of both halves of the mould, but there was no sign of a blemish. Since the gauge was wrong it was a pretty pointless exercise, but somehow he felt it was something he had to do.

'Describe to me how you cast a ball,' he said.

'I can do better than that, Inspector.' Bain retrieved the mould. 'I was about to make up a stock of shot when you arrived. You can watch if you want.'

Behind the small shooting gallery, and separated from it by a canvas sheet and beaded curtain doorway, was an even smaller work tent. Apart from a well singed and scarred table the only other item of importance was an upright portable wood-burning stove, on top of which sat an iron cauldron.

As Charlie watched, the grey liquid in the pot took on a darker hue and in the process acquired a slight bluish tone; it then took on a faint coppery blush before finally assuming the brilliance of mercury. Gripping the mould tightly in his left hand, Bain dipped his ladle into the molten lead and carefully transferred just enough to fill the ball cavity and the conical sprue. After waiting a few moments for the lead to solidify, he tapped open the small handle that cut the excess material from the bullet before swinging open the mould and allowing the shining ball to drop into a waiting bucket of cold water.

'It's the only way to make ends meet,' Bain stated. 'Can't afford to buy bullets, so I have to re-use every ball.'

'And no doubt some lead off the church

roof,' Charlie suggested, grinning.

'Not at all,' the man replied, clearly shocked. 'When I purchase lead it is only from genuine scrap dealers.'

This Charlie ignored. Instead he asked, 'What about the cartridges and caps?'

'Nothing I can do about the percussion caps,' Bain admitted ruefully. 'No choice but to buy them by the box. The cartridge cases, however, are a different thing. I make them out of the daily paper, as a matter of fact. I soak a strip of newsprint in potassium nitrate to make it completely combustible, wrap it round a wooden dowel of the right thickness, then glue the edge. After that I push the lead ball into one end and add the black powder to the tube.'

'More or less depending on whether you want the duck to fall or not,' Inspector Grant said.

'I have already admitted that,' Bain muttered. 'I thought we had an understanding.'

'And so we have.' Grant fished out his notebook and indulged in a bit of page-turning. 'All I require from you now is a bit of help in putting names to these initials. Start with W.B.. That might be you, Wesley Bain.'

'I suppose so, but it might just as well be William Blundell, the Hoopla man.' Bain looked confused. 'What is it all about?'

'Just answer the questions, Mr Bain. Did you ever borrow money from Gilbert Hayes?'

'Money lending? Is that what he was up to?'

'If you don't mind.'

'No, then,' Bain said. 'I live within my means, Inspector. I make a quid every day and at least three on a Saturday. Why would I want to borrow money?'

'Who can say? Maybe you're a gambler.'

Bain shook his head.

'A mug's game,' he said. 'You ask around. They'll tell you what chance you have.'

Charlie Grant pencilled in the name of William Blundell.

'S.H.?'

Bain gave it some thought.

'Sam Hicks,' he said at length. 'Photographic tent. Mothers can never resist having their kiddies' likenesses captured for posterity, though God alone knows why.'

'C.M.?'

'Clarence Moultrie. Phantasmagoria. Lantern slides for adult education.'

'Obscene pictures,' Grant suggested.

'But protected from you lot because it is instructive. Today it is The Dreadful Fate of Polly the Parlour-maid.'

'E.S.?'

'Emma Saunter, Princess of the Nile. Fortune Teller.'

'R.V.?'

'Rupert Vidler. Exhibits an embalmed mermaid from the South Pacific. Actually, it's a stuffed sea-lion with a monkey's head sewn onto it, but for Christ's sake don't tell him I said so. In fact, I would be obliged if you didn't tell any of them that I have given you information. There's a code of silence in these places as far as the coppers are concerned.'

'Then why are you helping me?'

'You know damned fine why. I need permission to buy black powder and percussion caps. You could take my livelihood away in five minutes.'

'I never threatened you with that.'

'You didn't have to.'

Charlie Grant ignored this.

'T.W.?' he asked.

'Thomas Weaver, knife thrower. He pays half a crown to anyone brave enough to risk the Spinning Wheel of Fire.'

'Many thanks,' Charlie Grant said. He returned his notebook and pencil to his capacious coat pocket. 'If you think of anything else, Mr Bain, or if you hear anything you think I should know, it'll always stand you in good stead.'

★ ★ ★

Currently the apple of Jake McGovern's eye and the most senior reporter on the *Advertiser*, Peter Rice was granted free rein to follow his own nose. If he didn't put in an appearance at the office for a few days, so be it. When he did turn up he would have something useful, something like the dredged-up sea chest, which McGovern immediately linked to the jade mask and turned into the curse yarn, which was now the talk of the city and increased the paper's circulation by a good twenty per cent. So it was a relaxed and self-satisfied Peter Rice who settled down in his attic dwelling in the Candleriggs to consider recent developments and figure out just how close he was to his great dream.

He now knew for certain that there were several treasure-hunters on the trail of the Jade King, but only the East African, Johannes Kirchner, and the American, Elisha Bradwell, seemed to be getting close. Of course they might have been following each other around in circles and just giving the impression of making progress, but that was extremely unlikely. Rice knew enough about these men and the way they operated to be fairly certain that they were doing all the right things in the right way.

This was supported by the fact that he

knew a few little details that they did not and could not, since he alone possessed the Holman account. Passed down through three generations, but seen only as a curiosity, it had first been jotted down by Lucius Holman, Rice's great-grandfather on his mother's side. While a warder on the male wing at the Garngad Asylum for the Insane, he had all the time in the world to absorb and give thought to the ravings of Tobias Fisher, who claimed to have stolen a great fortune, secreted it somewhere on his estate and murdered his manservant to silence forever the only witness to his villainy.

The only problem was the shortage of hard facts. No one could be sure that the man's name really was Fisher, or whether this was just one more imagining among many. And he was always vague about the nature of his treasure, claiming only that it consisted of eight boxes, containing in all the possessions of a king from a far-off land. As for the name of the estate, or the servant he was supposed to have murdered — no name, description or location ever passed his lips. In short, there was nowhere for a searcher to begin.

Nor did the nature of his insanity help. He reported seeing a ragged army of hollow-eyed, defeated men who had come at him through the thick walls of his house and hunted him. Corpse-like these creatures had shuffled along the many darkened corridors, targes raised and basket-hilted claybegs at the ready, until he was trapped, screaming, and unable to flee. Then other men came and buckled him up tightly so that he could not move his arms or legs. His last glimpse of the sky had been through the bars of the wagon that transported him to the madhouse.

The account, or such as there was of it, had meant little or nothing to Peter Rice until that wet night a year or so ago when, for no good reason other than being at a loss for something to do, he had wandered into the Mechanics Institute and attended a lecture given by the pathologist, Dr Hamilton, on the subject of a century-old murder of a man who had been wearing the shoes of a servant, and of the unusual nature of the weapon used to inflict the fatal blow. From that moment on, Rice had been obsessed with finding the possessions of a foreign king.

He rose from his seat, fetched his coiled chart from the narrow cupboard by the fire and took it to the table, where he spread it out and weighted down each corner with the books he kept there purely for that purpose.

Using a thin charcoal stick, he added yet another fact to the ever-growing mass of information. With only the legend of the

Nuestra Señora de Cartagena, the story of the ambush on the beach and Dr Hamilton's article in the *New York Science Review* to go on, Johannes Kirchner had located the shallow grave in which the murdered servant had been buried. Only the previous afternoon, Jake McGovern's favourite scratcher had lain on the top of the opposite wall of the gorge and followed Kirchner's every move through his three-draw, Lennie pocket telescope. But that was not all he saw. Not far away, but hidden from Kirchner's sight by the thick trees, Elisha Bradwell also followed his opponent's every move. It must have been as clear to the American, as it was to Rice himself, that the East African had figured out that the treasure of the Jade King was buried somewhere close to the servant's grave. But neither Kirchner nor Bradwell had the questionable benefit of the Holman account, in which the madman Fisher claimed to have secreted the boxes within his own property.

That advantage, Rice thought as he studied the chart, was one he might not be able to rely upon for much longer. For the first time he felt a growing sense of urgency, accompanied by a nagging thought that he was in danger of missing out entirely. These men, Kirchner and Bradwell, were professionals; he was not. In truth, he had no idea how quickly either one of them could achieve his objective once he had completed the preparation and knew exactly what he was going after. For all he, Peter Rice, knew the treasure might already have been located and spirited away.

Once this dread had firmly taken root nothing on earth could prevent him from stuffing his spyglasses into a large poacher-type pocket and quitting the place.

★ ★ ★

Now that her paying guests, or two of them at any rate, had retired to their respective rooms, and the maids were well out of harm's way up in their attic quarters, Elsie Maitland finally had a little time for herself, time she eagerly looked forward to each day because it was spent in the one part of the house that was truly hers, and where no one else might enter unless by invitation.

Ever since the day she married Ernest this had been her room of choice. Sharing a wall with the Flavel Kitchener and a large back boiler, the inner sanctum, which was entered by a narrow and discreet door at the foot of the stairs, was both dry and perpetually warm. Now the only slight drawback with opening the house to paying guests was that her best furniture now had to be stored, perhaps more tightly than she would have wished, in the large drawing room.

Yet restricting though her small world may have been, it lacked nothing for the provision of comfort. Though primarily a bedroom, it also served as an intimate parlour without any loss of propriety. Much of this had to do with the décor. The walls, apart from a broad, tan-coloured frieze, were covered in a hand-printed wallpaper, consisting of large floral scrolls in a deep cream over a background of a rich blue. Two chairs on either side of a low pedestal table were covered in fabric to match the wallpaper. There was clutter and no other furniture, except for her gleaming brass bed and her absolutely essential mahogany Duchess dressing table. Of all her possessions, Elsie was most fond of this piece, with its shaped mirror above three trinket drawers and its exquisite cabriole legs with platform base. When she herself was in service it was just such a boudoir table that she coveted above all else, because only the lady of the house could possibly possess such an item and have the time to spend in front of it.

As she sat there, waiting for that soft tap on the door, she reflected without remorse on the fact that she did not miss Ernest Maitland

and probably never had. It wasn't that kind of relationship. At her level marriage for love was a fiction found only in the Maid's Weekly. She desired security and freedom from the slavery of service. She imagined, without it being stated, that his motivation was lust. Better to satisfy the dark desires of one corn merchant than be at the mercy of landed toffs and their equally licentious and pompous underlings.

On reflection, there could be no doubt that she had seriously misjudged her husband. From the very start he had made it clear that he expected them to have separate rooms, and that any other arrangement was morally unacceptable. After a few chilly nights in the room now occupied by Elliot Stainer, he had crept downstairs to take advantage of the warmth of her chosen accommodation. Even so, and such as it was, any physical contact occurred in a state of total darkness. He never saw her naked, nor she him.

Worse, if asked to choose between the bed and the dining table, Ernest Maitland would have unashamedly plumped for the latter. And so it was that Elsie came to realize very early on that she had misread the man entirely in regard to his motives. He had wanted the best cook he could find, and the then Elsie Ross fitted the bill exactly. Not only a cook, but a professed cook at that, which meant that she had the ability to create an entire fancy banquet for as many guests as her lord and master wished to invite. There was little doubt that this fact tipped the scales in her favour and brought a twinkle to the eyes of the gluttonous Ernest Maitland.

Then came the gentle knock and, though fully anticipating it, Elsie experienced a pronounced flutter and even gave a light start as the knob turned and Henry Jarrett entered, closing the door silently behind him. For a few moments he just stood there, looking at her, admiring her, more than conscious of the fact that few women did not require a corset in order to keep a girlish, sylph-like form. Elsie, for her part, had always balked at the idea of tight-lacing, and of stays that required to be reinforced with whalebone and steel for the purpose of keeping the torso erect. It was all so unnecessary, since the whole tortuous process could be prevented in the first place.

But putting such admiration into words did not come easily to Jarrett. A generation or so earlier, men had felt comfortable with flowery phrases and gushing sentiment, but such outpourings were now far from the accepted norm. Indeed, they would be considered downright rakish, the honeyed talk of cads, tricksters and kept men. Self-respecting gentlemen like Superintendent Jarrett would sooner die than be thought of in that way.

'There is something I would like to discuss with you,' he said, conscious of the fact that it sounded stuffy and somewhat cold. Yet that was not how he had meant it. 'Perhaps I ought to have brought the subject up before, but with one thing or another . . . '

Although she could not imagine what he was about to say, she did have her suspicions — and her hopes — but somehow managed to remain calm as she rose from her chair and approached him.

'Henry,' she said softly, even though the other gentlemen were on the second floor and the maids might as well be in another land, 'the Jamaican coffee ought to be just right. You timed it perfectly.'

They took their places at the small pedestal table on which sat a silver tray with its matching coffee pot, sugar bowl and creamer. The pot, one of the few pieces Elsie and her late husband agreed upon, was of baluster form with leaf decoration and scrolled handle. Nothing was said while she poured two cups of the steaming dark liquid. By now there was no need to ask whether he wanted milk or sugar.

The Superintendent produced an envelope

from his inside pocket, raised the flap and smiled inwardly. Long experience of the fluctuating loyalties of servants in Hong Kong had led him to devise a simple but effective trick. When most people return a folded sheet to its cover they insert the fold first because it is easier to do. But not Jarrett. After reading the contents he would return the contents to the envelope with the fold uppermost. Upon checking the item later he discovered on several occasions that the letter had been removed, read and its intelligence no doubt conveyed to interested parties. This realization in turn led to the planting of false information and the breaking-up of several criminal organizations.

This time the tiny change was much less serious: one of the girls — and he had a pretty good idea which — had been tempted by the presence of the envelope on his mantelpiece, but had not observed his unusual way of replacing the fold. Yet he had no intention of reporting the incident to Elsie Maitland and getting the maid into trouble. That would be too petty.

'You really must forgive me, Elsie,' he said quietly, because it never did any harm to err on the side of caution. 'I certainly did not deliberately discount your views or willingly take you for granted.'

'I never for a moment thought you would,' Mrs Maitland said, her tone conspiratorial to match his. 'I have always known that there would be a discussion before the matter was finalized.'

'Matter?' Jarrett echoed.

'Yes, the property you consider to be most suitable.'

He looked down at the envelope and experienced a slight doubt with regard to who exactly had tampered with his mail. But just as quickly he expunged the thought from his mind. Elsie Maitland would never do such a thing. Of that he could be absolutely sure.

'You know about Largs?'

'I have supposed for some time that you were making enquiries about suitable villas, but I didn't know it was Largs.'

'Have you any objections?'

'No, none at all. It is not my place to object, if the circumstances are correct.'

'It goes without saying that the circumstances must be correct,' Jarrett said, 'but you must also like the house. Your feelings are all-important.'

Mrs Maitland smiled at this.

'They were not important when this property was purchased,' she admitted. 'It was fortunate that I took to the house so readily. I have known it to be otherwise.'

'That would not be acceptable as far as I am concerned.'

If Elsie had harboured even the slightest doubt, this concern for her feelings would have swept it away in an instant. Moreover, by even reading the letter he now held in his hand, she would be tacitly agreeing to share his house and his life.

She held out her hand and Jarrett surrendered the envelope. Then she withdrew the double fold, scanned it quickly and looked into his eyes in search of some indication of his own opinion. Jarrett, however, deliberately remained expressionless to force her to air her views.

'Very nice,' she said without any real conviction.

'One maid only?'

'No, no.' Elsie shook her head adamantly. 'Two girls are the very minimum required if we are to keep a respectable house.'

Henry Jarrett accepted the return of the letter and put it away in his inside pocket. In truth, the house in Largs was of no importance whatsoever. Its only real value was in obtaining Elsie's unqualified approval for their married life.

'It doesn't inflame me,' he said and was pleased to see her smile.

Without another word, Elsie rose quickly

from her chair and encircled the small table and resumed a sitting position, this time on Jarrett's lap.

'There is much to talk about,' she whispered, 'but I see no reason why our understanding should become public knowledge.'

*   *   *

Peter Rice hurried up the gaslit wooden stairway to his attic billet in the Candleriggs, locked the stout door behind him against a world of demons and took up a defensive position in the shadows beside the small window. From there he could see everyone who approached the building. Exactly what he intended to do if the monster came looking for him he had no idea besides a vague notion of keeping quiet and pretending there was no one in, while hoping that whatever it was would give up and go away.

He told himself that it was all in his mind, that there was no good reason why it should have followed him. To the best of his knowledge he had not been seen, yet the whole incident had been so bizarre and horrific that even he, unimaginative even cynical person that he was, found himself wondering if Jake McGovern's supernatural nonsense might not have a measure of truth in it. In his time Rice had written about dozens of murders, and had seen his share of bodies, but never before had he encountered anything as gory and brutal as the slaying he had witnessed by the light of the full moon from his vantage point in the woods.

Both the victim and the perpetrator were stark naked, the former unconscious and spread-eagled on a large tarpaulin, the latter standing over him with what appeared to be a flint dagger in his raised hand. Then, before Rice had a chance to fully comprehend the scene, the killer dropped swiftly to one knee, plunged the dagger into the prostrate man's belly, then cut him to the breastbone.

After that, everything was a bright and fractured nightmare, in which the murderer held aloft the bleeding heart and he, Peter Rice, crawled backwards over and through tangled brambles and sharp, painful twigs until he was sufficiently far away from the scene of the horror to be able to get to his feet and run for it.

The angular roofs of the tenements stood out against the first glow of dawn before Peter Rice finally persuaded himself that the devil was not coming to his home and that he was sufficiently safe for the time being to drag himself away from the window. He dropped into his armchair by the fire, but received little benefit from the dying embers. Not that it really mattered, of course. He was so numb that he had not even noticed the tear on the right knee of his trousers nor the scratches on his dirt-smeared fingers.

The events of the previous evening had started quietly, with no warning whatsoever of the hideous outrage that was to follow.

Having narrowed the search area by observing the professional hunters at work, and adding this information to the facts he had obtained by breaking into Dr Hamilton's files in the City Mortuary, it had become his nightly practice to secrete himself in the woods close to the place where the old skeleton had been found in the hope that either the East African or the Yank would exhibit a definite interest in one particular mansion over the others.

In a sense he felt perfectly justified in keeping an eye on their progress, for it was he who had anonymously furnished both men with the precise whereabouts of the old grave, in the hope that they would combine it with their own fund of deduced or acquired knowledge and thus lead him to the treasure.

What he had not anticipated was being reduced to cowering, feeling terrified, and being in fear of his very life.

5

Whenever Henry Jarrett foolishly congratu-
lated himself on having delegated all the cases
he had in hand, he inevitably found that soon
afterwards he had more work than he could
possibly cope with. As he leaned back in his
chair and shook open his paper, the indistinct
outline of a uniformed officer appeared at his
frosted glass door and he just knew that his
period of relaxation had come to an end.

The young constable rapped on the door,
received an order to enter, and appeared
almost immediately, but only from the neck
up.

'Excuse me, Superintendent,' he said over
Jarrett's paper, 'but Sergeant Black says to tell
you that a body has been found.'

'Where?'

'By the Govan Ferry, sir.'

'Floaters are found all the time, Constable,'
Jarrett offered. 'They are usually taken care of
by the Humane Society and the pathologist,
with only token police involvement, unless
there are suspicious circumstances.'

'I don't know anything about that,
Superintendent, but I believe it was Dr

Hamilton who requested your presence at the scene.'

Jarrett quickly folded the paper and dumped it on his blotter.

'Thank you, lad,' he said, getting to his feet. 'Better tell PC Jamieson to bring the wagonette round to the front.'

While the young constable sped off to carry out this important mission, Jarrett scribbled out a brief note in case Charlie Grant or Tommy Quinn should want to get in touch with him before he got back, then put on his coat, lifted his hat from the antler rack and set off at a moderate pace down the long corridor. He had a very good idea of just how long it would take Jamieson to bring Domino to the main entrance and he had no desire to be left standing on the pavement like something surplus to requirements.

In the event, the wagonette put in an appearance just as Tommy Quinn and young Walter Chapman got back from their visit to the university. Since this new matter took precedence over lost property, however valuable or interesting it might be, all three officers then boarded the vehicle and set off for the Govan Ferry.

★　★　★

116

In Henry Jarrett's room at 76 Delmont Avenue Lizzie Gill had finished making the bed when she noticed the torn envelope in the superintendent's pierced brass waste basket. Since Mrs Maitland was still busy in the kitchen, and the rhythmic beating of a carpet told her that Jeannie Craig was continuing to demonstrate how absolutely indispensable she was, Lizzie retrieved the fragments, noted that the letter itself had been inside the envelope when Henry Jarrett had ripped it up, and very quickly established that it was indeed the piece of correspondence that Jeannie had shown her.

More important, however, was the crumpled ball of blue writing paper which was also present in the bin. Once spread out, this revealed itself as a draft letter from Mr Jarrett to the house agent in Largs, thanking him for his kind service, but explaining that on this particular occasion it had been decided that the property was not exactly what was required.

At first, Lizzie felt compelled to rush down to the back yard and mock Jeannie for being wrong and working her cotton stockings off in a foolish demonstration of just how much Mrs Maitland needed her, but following on quickly came the much more appealing thought that it might be fun to keep this intelligence to herself entirely and let Miss

Craig beat herself into a froth for nothing. So she emptied the wastepaper bin into her pail, buried the evidence under a few shovelfuls of ash and took the whole thing down to the midden

* * *

Charlie Grant's first call was at the Hoopla stall run by William Blundell. This man turned out to be short, aggressive and disinclined to talk to the police.

'I had nothing to do with it,' he said sharply.

'Nothing to do with what?' Inspector Grant asked.

'Anything. I had nothing to do with anything.'

'Then why were your initials found in Gilbert Hayes's cash-book?'

'How do you know they are my initials?'

'I have exhausted all other possibilities as far as the showground is concerned.'

The man snorted derisively.

'By which you mean Wesley Bain,' he said. 'So you're going to believe him over me?'

'I don't believe anybody,' the inspector admitted. 'I'm investigating the murder of Gilbert Hayes and want to find out why certain people seem to have been paying him a regular amount every week.'

Blundell gave a pronounced shrug.

'There's nothing illegal about it,' he said softly, 'but it isn't something you want everyone to know, if you follow me.'

'Was it a loan?'

'Borrowed ten quid off him. Gave him at least twice that back again.' Suddenly, the man's bland expression yielded and he looked distinctly concerned. 'I wouldn't kill him for a few quid, if that's what you're thinking. I wouldn't kill anybody.'

'Somebody did,' Charlie Grant said flatly, 'and before I've finished here I'll know who it was. The best thing the guilty party can do is confess and explain the circumstances, because if he forces the court to prove his guilt there won't be anything between him and the gallows.'

Grant moved on then, but before tackling the next one on his list he spent a short time at a food stall, where he purchased a sliced sausage sandwich and a tin mug of black, unsweetened tea. That, he thought, should give the message enough time to pass along the grapevine and hopefully cause the guilty party to do something stupid, like making a run for it.

★ ★ ★

The hand-operated chain ferry had carried passengers and horse-dawn vehicles between Pointhouse on the northern side of the river and Govan on the southern for the previous one hundred and thirty years. Recently, the Clyde Navigation Trust had announced their intention of replacing it with a larger, steam-driven vessel, but that was still a couple of years off at the very least.

As PC Jamieson drew Domino to a halt and hunted out his clay jaw-warmer, the three detectives alighted from the wagonette and made their way down the slope to a small and somewhat rickety hut about a dozen yards from the water's edge, where Dr Hamilton and two uniformed officers were waiting for them. Jamieson, though happy in his job as police driver, was always more interested in the live world than the dead one, and in particular how other men plied their trades and earned their corn. On this occasion he found himself quickly and completely fascinated by the way the ferry operated; a long chain was firmly attached at both sides of the river and passing through a windlass on the vessel, but lay for the most part on the bottom so as not to snag normal water-born traffic. By cranking the handle the ferryman caused his boat to traverse between shores countless times every day.

When Henry Jarrett reached the ramshackle hut Dr Hamilton took him by the arm and led him to one side.

'This is delicate matter, Superintendent,' he whispered. 'If possible, I would like to keep it between ourselves.'

Jarrett raised an eyebrow.

'The boy is untried,' Jarrett answered softly, 'but Sergeant Quinn — '

'Please, bear with me,' Hamilton said. 'Admit them to the murder scene if you must, but take what I say with a pinch of salt. I'll tell you the real story when we get to the mortuary, and then I think you will understand what I mean.'

The dead man was completely naked. He lay on his back on the old plank floor, his legs together and his arms by his sides. But for the hideous gash on his abdomen and his pallid colour he might have been at rest.

'Killed elsewhere,' Hamilton stated casually. 'The blood loss would have been considerable, but there is scarcely a drop on the timber.'

'Has he been here long?' Jarrett asked.

Dr Hamilton dropped to one knee and raised the corpse just enough for them to see the dark underside caused by the setting of the remaining blood.

'Judging by the lividity,' he said, 'I would

venture to say late yesterday evening. I think we can be reasonably sure that it was after the ferryman finished for the day. I am told that the boat runs until nine o'clock at this time of year.'

'Some sort of vehicle must have been used,' Jarrett observed, 'but there are no cart tracks around this hut.'

'The slope is too steep to turn a cart,' Tommy Quinn observed. 'It must have halted up there where PC Jamieson is now and the body carried down here.'

Jarrett nodded his agreement.

'Do you concur, Dr Hamilton?' he enquired. 'Could a single killer have man-handled the corpse down here, or would it have taken two?'

In response Hamilton lifted one of the dead man's legs and let them see the muddy heels and calves.

'One man pulling him by the armpits,' he said, 'or two dragging his arms. But one thing is for sure, between the ferryman who found the body this morning and the beat constable he hailed, all traces of the killer's boot prints have been well and truly churned to mud.'

'Pity about that,' said Jarrett.

'More than a pity, Superintendent. You know, you are really going to have to educate the uniform branch in how to avoid mangling evidence.'

'It is a delicate situation, Dr Hamilton. The uniform and detective branches don't exactly see eye to eye.'

'I am fully aware of that, but until they learn how to behave at a crime site my job, and yours, will continue to be more difficult than it needs to be.'

Sergeant Quinn glanced at young Chapman to see how he was taking this criticism, but far from looking abashed the boy was nodding his full agreement.

Anxious to change the subject, Jarrett said, 'A single knife cut, Doctor?'

Hamilton caught his eye and was clearly warning him not to press too hard at this stage.

'Very probably,' he said at length, but he was lying.

Taking the hint, Jarrett said, 'Identification is not going to be easy. Any indicators?'

'One,' Hamilton said, 'if you could call it that. At first I thought it was total robbery — all clothes and all possessions — but this ring was on his left hand so that pretty well rules out murder for theft.'

Henry Jarrett accepted the object and considered it closely. It was gold and extremely ornate. Within the claw was a blue stone on which had been engraved a tiny crucifixion scene, with a fine sunburst above the Christ figure.

'Constable,' he said, handing the piece to Walter Chapman, 'you were in the jewellery trade. What do you make of this?'

The Acting DC was initially surprised at being so consulted, but quickly resumed his composure and gave the item his full attention. Officers were not born into the force; all had been in previous employment elsewhere, and it was Jarrett's practice to make use of whatever expertise they may have had. The boy had been a jeweller's assistant before the tragic murder of Abel Hind in his shop in the Argyle Arcade had left him unemployed and with no career prospects. It had been Henry Jarrett who suggested that he should join the police, and for this reason the superintendent had taken an interest in the young man's progress. In particular, Jarrett was struck by his powers of observation and interest in technology, which he felt would be of use to the Detective Department and wasted on the beat.

'I am no expert, Superintendent,' Walter offered, 'but I can tell you that it is old. Spanish, I think. It appears to have the Cordoba hallmark, although much of that is worn away.'

'And the stone?'

'A blue sapphire, sir. Flawed, of course.'

'So it is relatively worthless?'

'On the contrary, Superintendent. The flaw increases the value of a sapphire. But that also depends on the carat and depth of colour of the stone.'

Jarrett gave this some thought.

'Have you ever sold such an object?' he asked.

'No, never. Mr Hind wasn't in that class, sir. Not many jewellers are. They used to meet up every morning in the coffee shop to discuss business, but never once did Mr Hind say anything to me about a flawed sapphire. If this piece had ever been offered to one of the jewellers the news would have been round the Arcade like wildfire.'

'Nevertheless,' Jarrett said, 'I want you to take the ring and get along to the Argyle Arcade. Confirm your opinion of it and see if any of the jewellers can add anything of interest. I'll be perfectly frank with you, lad. Much as I would like additional information, I am also doing this to give you a bit of experience and responsibility. Just remember not to tell them where you got it.'

★　★　★

Charlie Grant pushed back the flap of the large tent and stepped inside. Fortunately, for him at any rate if not for the photographer, there were no customers at that time of the day.

'Sam Hicks?' he said.

'Sir.' The thin moustachioed man laid his newspaper aside and got to his feet. 'You will be the police inspector.'

'Word gets around.'

'It does indeed. This is a very tight community.'

'Friendly?'

'Not necessarily.' Hicks indicated the free chair. 'Please take a seat, Inspector. You must be on your feet a lot.'

Charlie was not entirely sure if this was courtesy or sarcasm.

'Mr Hicks,' he continued, producing his notebook, 'it would save a great deal of time if you would describe to me the nature of your dealings with Gilbert Hayes.'

Hicks smiled thinly.

'I didn't shoot him,' he said.

'No one is suggesting you did, but somebody shot him, so it's a simple process of elimination. Now, what was your connection with the deceased?'

'I borrowed money from him.'

'For?'

'That camera beside you, Inspector. It is a sliding-box type dry collodion plate camera with a stereoscopic lens. People pay good money for stereoscopic images now and I didn't want to miss out.'

'Why did you have to go to Gilbert Hayes for the money?'

'That is easily answered. I am not a careful man when it comes to money, Inspector. I have a weakness.'

'The ladies?'

Hicks laughed.

'God, no,' he said. 'Four-legged fillies. Sadly, I can't pick them.'

'Then how did you manage to repay him at the rate of two pounds per week?'

'You are well informed, sir. The truth is I can take in five or six pounds on a Saturday afternoon, so Hayes always made a point of popping round here while I was still flush and before I had managed to get rid of it. That was how he operated, you see. He knew the best time to pounce. If he had waited for any of us to turn up at his van with the money he would still have been sitting there waiting for hell to freeze over.'

'Didn't he enforce matters?' Charlie asked.

'No. Small lenders don't. It isn't worth it for them to hire hooligans. Truth is, borrowing is a regular, ongoing thing. If you don't repay you don't get another sub.'

'And people like Hayes are your only options?'

'Inspector, banks don't lend money to travellers, because we would travel and they would whistle for it.'

At that moment a woman swept into the tent with a small, unco-operative boy in tow. Charlie Grant got quickly to his feet and said, 'We'll make that do for the time being, Mr Hicks. If there is anything else I require I know where to find you.'

'Always happy to oblige, sir.'

* * *

It had been Dr Hamilton's intention to impart his findings to Jarrett alone, but he had dealt with Tommy Quinn on several occasions and knew how much the superintendent trusted the young Irishman.

After the porters had transferred the naked corpse from their iron stretcher to the large marble slab, they took their leave and discreetly closed the mortuary door behind them. Hamilton gave them a few moments, then took a quick look out to make sure that no one was loitering in the long, white-tiled corridor.

'Actually, I was about to get in touch with

you on another matter, Superintendent,' he said softly, 'but that can wait for the moment.'

'As you wish, Doctor. What can you tell me about this individual?'

'I can tell you that Jake McGovern has a great deal to answer for. I hold that man to be personally responsible for this.'

Jarrett knew better than to question Dr Hamilton's judgement, especially as it was clear that he was in possession of some as yet undisclosed information.

'You said something about telling me the real story earlier, Doctor,' he said. 'Presumably it is not entirely as it appears.'

'Precisely so.' Hamilton lifted a small wooden pill box which he opened to reveal a nest of cotton wool on which lay a small fragment of stone. 'What do you think this is?'

Jarrett and Quinn exchanged a brief glance. Then the Irishman suggested, 'A piece of flint?'

'Agreed,' Jarrett said. 'It looks like a piece of flint.'

'That is exactly what it is,' Hamilton affirmed. 'It is the point of a flint knife used to cut open the victim. At first I thought it had been accidentally introduced into the body when this poor fellow was being shifted hither and thither and generally manhandled, but then I suddenly realized what it really was.'

'Are you suggesting that the stabbing of this man is somehow linked to the jade mask and McGovern's nonsense about a curse?' This from Jarrett.

'Not just linked, Superintendent, a direct consequence of it. And he wasn't stabbed.' Dr Hamilton reached inside the abdomen of the corpse and brought out the bloody heart: 'He was sacrificed.'

Jarrett was horrified.

'Are you serious?'

'Never more so.'

'Then we are looking for a lunatic.'

'I am not altogether sure if that is true.' Hamilton placed the organ in a tin dish and washed his hands in the deep sink. 'A fanatic, perhaps, but madness is a very difficult condition to define.'

'What level of skill would be required, Dr Hamilton?' Tommy Quinn asked. 'Is this the work of a surgeon, for example?'

'Not at all. There would be virtually no medical expertise required. Anyone who knew how the priests used to perform such sacrifices could do it, provided he had a strong stomach.' Hamilton lifted his scalpel and held it, dagger-like, over the gaping wound. 'Would you like me to demonstrate the process?'

'I am not sure that the word 'like' is appropriate, Doctor,' Jarrett said honestly, 'but please do.'

'Very well. But first let me dispel a common myth. When most people read about the heart being removed they imagine some kind of great circular cut being made on the chest. It isn't like that. The knife was first driven into the abdomen, then a upward cut is made through the thoracic diaphragm, which is a sheet of muscle that extends across the bottom of the rib cage. The purpose of this diaphragm is to separate the thoracic cavity from the abdominal cavity. Having done this, our assailant was able to reach inside the rib cage and tear out the still beating heart, which in religious ceremonies would have been placed in a receptacle as an offering to the gods. Our self-appointed high priest no doubt performed this offering ceremony before returning the heart to the body for us to find.'

'Why?'

'I am not a mind-doctor, Superintendent, but I assume it is by way of a challenge. He is cocking a snook at you, or whoever is trying to catch him.'

'I thought you said he wasn't insane.'

'He doesn't have to be. Not in the gibbering sense of the word. Supreme self-confidence would be enough.'

'Is that why he left the ring behind?'

Dr Hamilton nodded, grinning.

'I was about to come to that,' he said. 'I suppose it was his way of letting us know that the motive definitely wasn't robbery. Although there is another possible explanation.'

'And that is?'

'It is a Christian image. He speaks to other gods. I dare say it was a choice between destroying it and using it to bait us. He chose the latter.'

'You know, Dr Hamilton,' Jarrett observed, 'for a man who isn't a mind-doctor you do very well indeed.'

'One acquires bits and pieces of knowledge over the years. We have encountered supreme egotists before and they always make a mistake sooner or later.'

'Indeed they do, and let us hope that this one makes it sooner rather than later. Preferably before the Chief Constable returns to his desk.' After a brief pause, Jarrett continued, 'Can we be sure there is only one killer?'

'Not absolutely, but the victim was struck on the rear of the head behind the right ear. I think the reason for that may have been to render him unconscious and incapable of putting up a fight. You see, traditionally five priests would have been involved, one holding each wrist and each ankle of the conscious, partly drugged victim, and a high priest who performed the actual sacrifice. The blow to the head suggests one murderer working alone or two at the most, but I really can't be sure.'

'Yes, I quite understand,' Jarrett said, then went on, 'You said there was another matter that might interest us, Doctor.'

'Yes, the glyph.'

'Sorry?'

Instead of replying immediately, Dr Hamilton crossed to his mahogany shelves and returned with a strawboard box, which he placed on the table normally reserved for the victim's clothes and personal belongings, but which was empty on this occasion since the corpse was already naked. The box contained an entire skeleton and a few assorted items found in close proximity.

'You probably won't remember this, Superintendent,' he said, flicking through the loose papers. 'A little over a year ago a plant collector came upon a human skull protruding from what turned out to be a shallow grave. The police were sent for, of course, but soon lost interest when I demonstrated that the crime, for a crime it most certainly was, had taken place more than a century ago.'

'Kelvin Vale,' Tommy Quinn put in quickly. 'Inspector Grant and I were in attendance on that occasion, but since it never became a case no file was opened on it.'

'It was not an open case then,' Dr Hamilton offered, 'perhaps now it may become part of one.'

'Forgive me, Doctor,' Henry Jarrett said, 'but I fail to see . . . '

'Just bear with me, Superintendent.' Hamilton lifted the skull and displayed the gaping hole on the crown. 'Typical of a single, devastating blow to the head, causing instant death. I have the missing section in the form of twenty-seven pieces, which I intend to reassemble someday but so far haven't had the time.

'But it isn't the wound that is truly fascinating, it is this.' He replaced the skull in the box and selected instead a large piece of lead sheet, curved to fit over a man's shoulder. This he placed briefly over his own right shoulder, as if to justify what he was about to say. 'Imagine for a moment that you are lowering heavy objects, and that you are doing so by letting out a rope that extends over your shoulder and is being controlled by your free hand. It wouldn't be long before the rope cut into your shoulder and if it slipped sideways it might even cause painful burns or a bloody gash on the side of your neck. So to avoid that, you drape a piece of lead or heavy cow hide over your shoulder. If you look closely at this you will see the lines caused by the rope, but you will see something else as well. Note the circular dent in the soft metal.'

'It appears to have a pattern of sorts in it,' Jarrett suggested.

'Exactly. I believe that it was caused by a war club.'

'Like an African knobkerrie?'

'Of similar size and weight, but this one was engraved with a complex image.' Dr Hamilton put down the metal shoulder protector and unfolded a thin paper square. 'I made what was effectively a brass rubbing from the impression in the lead, Superintendent, and this is the result.'

Henry Jarrett frowned pensively as he studied the strange image, but it was Sergeant Quinn who spotted it first.

'The jade mask,' he said. 'This is the round-cornered square that's on the forehead of the green man-serpent.'

'Larger,' Jarrett agreed, 'and not quite by the same artist.'

'No, but it is supposed to be the same subject.' Quinn looked quizzically at Hamilton. 'Is this just a coincidence, Doctor?'

'I very much doubt that, Sergeant. Unfortunately, not enough is known about glyphs, as they call them, but there is no doubt in my mind that the weapon used to kill this man more than a hundred years ago was directly linked to your mask.' Dr Hamilton took back his heel ball rubbing, returned it to the box and proceeded to unwrap a small piece of cloth, exposing as he did so a pair of metal buckles. 'Let me tell you the whole story, gentlemen. It may or may not be of some assistance in your search for the modern day high priest.

'As you said, Sergeant, it was finding these objects in the shallow grave that put paid to any police interest in the matter. They are in fact shoe buckles from a period long before our time. I was able to say this with absolute certainty, since they are made of pinchbeck, an alloy of zinc and copper, which was used as a cheap imitation of gold. Also, they are some one and a half inches in width and completely undecorated. Thus my researches told me that they were from the shoes of a servant of the highest rank and were made after 1733 and before 1760. You will have to take my word for this.

'Now for the weapon that struck the fatal blow. Without the help of the lead shoulder protector, the best I could have said was that the man was killed by a sizeable, near-spherical object. This could have been a large sea-washed pebble of the sort popular with gardeners, who use them to edge pathways and so forth. But the image on the lead sheet really provided me with a fuller picture.

'Imagine a ball about the size of a grapefruit, possibly of stone and richly decorated with a deeply incised pattern. It would be attached to a wooden shaft like any other war club, but this one was not meant to be used by a common soldier. From the Ancient Egyptians up to our own Crown Jewels there has generally been at least one mace in monarchical regalia, and this is no exception.

'What I think happened is as follows. For some reason we will never fully understand, the servant was pursued by someone wielding the war club. Finally, the one who was desperate to put him to death managed to strike his right shoulder, breaking the clavicle, or collar bone, and undoubtedly driving him to his knees. The second and fatal blow was downwards to the top of the head and delivered with great force. The corpse was then buried at a depth of about two feet, but the mace, or club, was not interred with him. In my opinion the murderer knew full well the value of the ceremonial weapon and had no intention of losing it.'

'How many people have heard this story?' Jarrett asked.

'Unfortunately, too many, Superintendent. Not long after the finding of the skeleton I gave a talk on the subject at the Mechanic's Institute. This was very well received and encouraged me to write a piece for the *New York Science Review*, which included an engraving of the glyph on the supposed mace. I am now somewhat concerned that I may have inadvertently provided the tinder to which Jake McGovern has added the spark.'

After a few moments, Henry Jarrett said, 'Are you saying, Doctor, that your article on the skeleton and the glyph mark on the lead shoulder plate may have brought about the ritual murder we now have to contend with.'

'That is more or less correct; I believe that my account may have attracted certain elements to the city, but, until the picture of the jade mask carrying the same image was published in the *Advertiser*, these people could not be certain that they were on the right track.'

'To find the treasure chest?'

'Eight chests, sir,' Tommy Quinn corrected. 'According to Professor Greenaway at the university.'

'Quite so,' Jarrett conceded, 'but it is one

thing to seek lost treasure and another to perform appalling acts like this.'

'Unless it's a warning, Superintendent,' Sergeant Quinn suggested. 'McGovern's curse story could have given one of these treasure hunters an idea of how to scare off the competition.'

'Possibly, but only the small fry. I can't imagine any serious hunter being unnerved by the likes of this, however gory it may be,' Jarrett said, adding, 'Right now what we need most is a name for this fellow. Let us hope that young Chapman has some luck with the ring.'

'One last thing,' Dr Hamilton offered as the detectives were taking their leave. 'Not long after my lecture at the Mechanic's Institute this building was broken into and my files were rifled. I don't know if the crook got everything he was looking for, because he was disturbed in the act by the watchman and showed a clean pair of heels.'

'Have you any idea what he was seeking?'

'I think so, but I can't be absolutely sure. At no time in the lecture or my article for the *New York Science Review* did I say where the skeleton was found. One of the buff folders the intruder removed from the cabinet and had been examining on the table contained just such information.'

There was no particular reason why Acting Detective Constable Walter Chapman should have chosen 'J. Meyer's' over all the other jewellery shops in the Argyle Arcade, other than from the fact that it was closer to the Buchanan Street entrance of the glass-covered, L-shaped shopping walkway. When he was a junior with Mr Hind most of the shops were held in high regard. This was particularly true of Mr Meyer's, who had a carriage trade that was the envy of all the others. Having decided that he would be more likely to get the answers he wanted there, he pressed on the large brass bar and entered the world of the wealthy.

'Of course I remember you, young Chapman,' Mr Meyer said sadly. 'Terrible business, that. The death of Abel Hind shook the trade to its very foundations.'

'It's still fresh,' Walter offered.

'Indeed it is.' Mr Meyer nodded his agreement. 'And who would have expected you to join the constabulary?'

Not quite clear how to take that, Walter merely produced the ring and requested as much information as the elderly gentleman could provide.

Mr Meyer, for his part, accepted the object

and studied it reverently, then placed it on his mahogany-covered counter and for half a minute or so he merely stood there, staring at it.

'Presumably you are not offering it for sale,' he said. 'Great pity. I should like to acquire it.'

'It's not mine to sell,' Walter said, quite unnecessarily. 'It's evidence.'

'And what happens when it ceases to be evidence?'

'If a true and lawful heir to this piece cannot be traced, I should imagine it will be sold along with everything from the Lost Property store. If I remember right, that's every six months.' In a desire to get back on track, Walter said, 'What can you tell me about it, Mr Meyer?'

'You have had a few years' experience, lad,' Meyer said, smiling. 'Tell me what you know of it.'

'Well, it's a flawed sapphire, engraved with the crucifixion. The ring itself is gold, of course, and appears to be Spanish, probably hallmarked in Cordoba. I would think it is very old.'

'And you would be absolutely correct, Walter. Very good indeed. The stone is a star sapphire and the engraving is second to none. As you say, the hallmark is Cordoban and the gold is very probably from the New World.'

'Can you date the style?'

'Possibly early seventeenth century.' Mr Meyer reluctantly handed the ring back, adding, 'I know that you are not permitted to tell me anything about the circumstances surrounding the piece, Walter, but I would venture to suggest that it was almost certainly found within recent memory.'

'How can you be sure of that, Mr Meyer?'

'I am not sure, but I can assure you that it has never been sold publicly within my professional lifetime. It may have changed hands privately, of course, but if it had ever appeared in an auction catalogue I and many like me would have spotted it instantly.'

'Could you put a price on it?'

'I wouldn't begin to guess. What I will say is this. I know at least two people who would buy it from me sight unseen.'

6

By the time Charlie Grant got back to headquarters he felt that he knew less than when he started. As expected, Clarence Moultrie, Emma Saunter, Rupert Vidler and Thomas Weaver all admitted to having borrowed money from the deceased man, Gilbert Hayes, while denying having anything whatsoever to do with his untimely demise.

'I have left Williamson and Russell to interview everything that moves, except the animals,' Grant said, 'but quite frankly, Superintendent, there isn't much to go on. And to make matters worse, doubts have been cast on Dr Hamilton's estimate regarding time of death.'

Henry Jarrett reflected surprise. This was not a commonplace occurrence. Tommy Quinn, for his part, found it sufficiently intriguing to give it his full attention.

'How so?' Jarrett asked.

'One of them, Rupert Vidler — a thorough-going rogue who exhibits a so-called embalmed mermaid, which is actually a stuffed sea-lion, onto which he has sewn the head of a monkey — swears that he saw Gilbert Hayes walking away from the fairground at a time considerably after that at which Dr Hamilton estimated the murder occurred. As well as sporting large check trousers and a green coat, Hayes had a jaunty way of walking and wore his hat very much at an angle.'

'And the other contradictory account?'

'The knife-thrower, Thomas Weaver, could clearly see Hayes's caravan from his booth and is equally adamant that our victim entered his wagon when, according to Dr Hamilton, he should have been dead.'

'Obviously, they are either mistaken or lying, Inspector,' Sergeant Quinn suggested. 'Or else the killer was deliberately deceiving them after he had disposed of Gilbert Hayes. It wouldn't be too difficult to impersonate a man's style of walking or dress in a similar fashion.'

'And Hayes' home was ransacked,' Jarrett added. 'That proven fact supports the eyewitness's account of someone entering the caravan.'

Inspector Grant acknowledged this with a slight shrug. Ever since the superintendent had informed him of the sacrificial victim, the killing at the fairground had paled by comparison: he was beginning to feel as though he had drawn the short straw.

'Do you want me to stick with it, sir?' he asked.

'Difficult to say, Inspector. Neither case holds out much promise of a swift conclusion. Young Chapman's visit to the Argyle Arcade added nothing to our fund of knowledge. What we need in both cases is fresh information, freely offered.'

★ ★ ★

It was a thoroughly miserable and utterly forlorn Albert Sweetman who huddled, cross-legged on the narrow bed in the Dark Glen Inn, a single blanket draped over his head and around his shoulders. He was trapped in the back of beyond and no one in the civilized world knew of his plight.

There was no doubt whatsoever in his mind that the McCreedy woman was mad, but that did not help. The knowledge that she was of unsound mind while in possession of a percussion fowling piece was not a great comfort, and represented a more immediate threat to his well being than either Reverend Gillen or Sergeant Clarke. So he decided that Mother McCreedy had to be pacified, short of actually going along with her insane plans to snare a comfortable son-in-law by abduction and threats.

Several times in the last hour or so he thought he had heard her approaching his tiny room at the end of the long corridor, but on each occasion she had turned on her heels and returned from whence she came. If she was trying to unnerve him she was making a good job of it.

Finally, inevitably, she paused outside his door and his heart missed a beat or two when the key was turned in the lock.

'I brought you something to eat,' Mrs McCreedy said coldly, placing a pewter plate and utensils on the small table. The gun was still present, but cracked now and slung in the crook of her left arm. That, however, was no help and certainly not an incentive to flee. Even if he could get past her and out of the room, the passageway was long and narrow and his chance of getting to the stairs without receiving a load of buckshot in the back was almost non-existent.

'Thank you,' he mumbled, hoping it sounded suitably respectful. 'I'll enjoy that.'

'Shut up!' she ordered, glaring at him. 'Have you made your mind up? Is it to be the minister or the law?'

'Actually . . . ' Sweetman began.

'Enough of the stalling! I want your answer now. Are you going to make a decent woman out of her or not? Do I send for Mr Gillen or Sergeant Clarke?'

'That's what I would like to discuss with

you, my dear lady.'

'There's nothing to discuss, and I'm neither your dear nor a lady.'

'Come come, now, you do yourself an injustice.'

'I'll do you a mischief if there's any more shilly-shallying.' Mrs McCreedy snapped the piece closed and swung the muzzle in his direction. 'Do I fetch Reverend Gillen or are you to be taken to Fort William in irons?'

'One moment,' Sweetman said, his palms raised and open in a gesture of surrender, 'let me make a suggestion. If you permit me to return to Glasgow to sort out my financial affairs, I will be back on the very next steamer and go through with whatever ceremony you require.'

'Do you think I'm stupid? If I let you go I'll never see you again, you fat beast. I am of a mind to shoot you right now for having the gall to take me for a simpleton.'

A panic-stricken Albert Sweetman managed to somehow get himself deeper into the corner, his knees drawn up as far as his stomach would permit in a vain attempt at staving off the coming blast.

'All right!' he squealed. 'It was a stupid mistake. I'll marry her, if that's what you want.'

'That's what I want.'

'And if that's what she wants.'

'What does it matter what she wants? She needs to marry well, but if left to her own judgement she'd make a bad match. That's for sure. Now, you may not be much to look at, but you've got money enough to look after her and me the way we've always wanted.'

'Her and you?' Sweetman said, parrot-like.

'There's nothing wrong with your hearing.' Mrs McCreedy closed in on him. She was grinning now. 'With a bit of luck your heart won't be so strong.'

★　★　★

As was so often the case when no leads presented themselves in the normal course of things, the Fates intervened, and the wheels of justice once more began to turn.

The first break literally had Inspector Grant's name on it. The small envelope had been sealed with wax on the flap, but had not been posted; the boy who surrendered it to Sergeant Black at the front desk had turned on his heels and fled before he could be questioned.

Charlie Grant accepted the item from a young constable sent by Davie Black, broke the red wax blob with his thumbnail and withdrew the single sheet of paper. Superintendent Jarrett and Detective Sergeant Tommy Quinn watched the process with interest, while waiting to be enlightened.

'It would seem that someone is less than partial to Wesley Bain,' Charlie Grant said, placing the open fold in front of his chief. 'According to this, Bain shot and killed Gilbert Hayes, and furthermore the murder weapon is hidden in the shooting booth.'

'Then you had better look into the matter, Inspector,' Jarrett said, a faint smile on his lips. 'But I would tread carefully if I were you. The anonymous writer knows too much.'

⋆ ⋆ ⋆

Wesley Bain half-expected Inspector Grant's return, if only because it was too much to ask for that he should have finished his enquiries and returned from whence he came. To be confronted by both the senior officer and two burly detectives from the lower rank, however, was more than Bain had expected.

'Certain information has come our way,' Charlie Grant said. 'We are going to have to search your stall and caravan.'

Bain was momentarily at a loss for words.

'Do you have a warrant?' he managed, but it was little more than a pathetic whisper.

'Do we need one? If you have nothing to hide surely you have no objection to co-operating with us?'

'No, not at all.' The stallholder raised the wooden flap and stepped aside to allow them into his booth. 'I just don't know what you're looking for.'

'You'll know soon enough when we find it.' The Inspector indicated the barrel full of broken and twisted lead. DC Williamson began to remove the soft metal a piece at a time and lay it on the counter. DC Russell, for his part, concentrated on the side-shelves that held the prizes, such as they were. 'Do you have someone who will look after your business for a spell, Mr Bain?'

Wesley Bain was visibly stunned by this.

'Are you arresting me?' he asked.

'It may come to that.' Charlie Grant held out a hand and accepted the bullet mould the detective constable had found beneath the grey fragments. He then flicked open the sprue lever and drew the handles apart. Even without the benefit of a magnifying glass he could see the tell-tale triangular blemish. Yet he said nothing more until Ian Williamson unearthed the pistol. 'I think perhaps we should continue this conversation at headquarters, Mr Bain.'

★ ★ ★

Henry Jarrett's break came in the form of a small, dumpy lady with a tight bonnet and a crocheted bag. Judging by her neat appearance and quiet, unassuming manner this was very probably the first time she had ever been inside a police station.

Numerous men went missing from domestic environments every day, and many more from lodging-houses when they found it impossible to pay the rent. But this particular vanished gentleman had taken nothing with him, had paid a month in advance, and was, in the lady's opinion, a sober, considerate, model guest.

Although Sergeant Black received several such reports daily, most of which were resolved by the return of the subject of the report, there was something in the lady's concerned demeanour that caused this particular case to stand out from the crowd. So rather than dismiss her with the usual assurances that all would no doubt turn out fine, he escorted her to Superintendent Jarrett's office, explained the situation, and returned to his duties at the front desk.

Jarrett bade the lady take a seat, then took his rightful place behind the large desk and pressed the button for Detective Sergeant Quinn.

'Mrs . . . ?'

'Hyslop,' she said, clearly eager to co-operate in every way. 'Jemima. My address is 94 Benton Mews, off the Great Western Road.'

'Superintendent Jarrett,' he offered, then the glazed door opened and closed almost soundlessly and Tommy Quinn positioned himself in the corner. 'This is Detective Sergeant Quinn. Please tell us what you told the uniformed sergeant.'

'Well, it concerns my lodger, Mr Kirchner. He left the house after dinner yesterday evening and did not return.'

'Is that unusual?'

'Unprecedented, Superintendent. Johannes Kirchner has been with me now for over five months and not once has he ever put a foot wrong, as the expression goes.'

'Is he in the habit of going out at night?'

'He regularly takes an evening stroll, but never for more than an hour or so. He is a very studious man, Superintendent, and not given to levity or fancies.'

Jarrett considered this.

'The name sounds foreign, Mrs Hyslop. Is he German?'

'East African, I believe, although he doesn't talk a great deal about himself or his business.'

'And what might that be?'

'You know, I really don't know. All I can

say for sure is that he does not seem to have a place of work, and his times are somewhat irregular. He comes and goes whenever it suits him, and sometimes he does not leave the house for days at a time.' Mrs Hyslop leaned forward as though imparting a confidence. 'I am of the opinion that he may be a writer of sorts, but I would not like it known that I am talking behind his back.'

'Only out of necessity, Mrs Hyslop, Mr Kirchner is missing and you are clearly concerned. You did the right thing in coming forward.' Jarrett paused briefly, then said, 'Perhaps you should give us a description of the gentleman.'

'I am afraid there is nothing particularly outstanding about him, Superintendent. Other than his pronounced accent, that is.'

'Height?'

'Average, I would say.'

'Is he slim, heavy?'

'Once more, I would have to say average. I know it isn't very helpful, but I don't know what else to say.'

'Hair, then. What colour is that?'

'Oh, that is different. Light sandy, I would say.' Mrs Hyslop thought for a moment before adding, 'I almost forgot the eyes. He has very light blue eyes. I remember thinking how striking they were when I first met him.'

Jarrett glanced at Tommy Quinn. There was no question in either of their minds that the body in the mortuary was anything other than the mortal remains of Johannes Kirchner.

Henry Jarrett drew open a drawer, removed a folded blue cloth square and opened it on the blotter where the lady could clearly see it.

'Do you recognize this ring, Mrs Hyslop?' he asked.

Jemima Hyslop again leaned forward, this time for a closer look. Then she nodded.

'This is Mr Kirchner's,' she said softly. 'It is quite outstanding. Indeed he told me it was unique.'

Jarrett folded the cloth around the object and returned it to the drawer.

'Much as it pains me to say this, Madam,' he said, 'I must tell you that your lodger, Johannes Kirchner, is dead.'

Mrs Hyslop stared at him for a few moments, then nodded and gave out a long sigh.

'I thought you were going to say that, Superintendent,' she admitted. 'In fact, I think I suspected as much when he didn't return to the house.'

'Is there any sound reason for fearing that?'

She shrugged lightly.

'The gun,' she said.

Jarrett frowned and out of the side of his eye saw DC Quinn launch himself away from the wall to stand erect and ready for whatever orders his chief had in mind.

'Tell me about the gun,' Jarrett said softly.

'He kept it under his mattress,' Mrs Hyslop confided. 'Sometimes when he went out he would take it with him. When he failed to return I checked and it was missing.'

'I don't suppose you know what sort of gun it was, Madam?' Jarrett enquired.

'It was just a gun, Superintendent.'

'Yes, of course.' After a few seconds Jarrett went on, 'Not really in keeping with his being a writer, is it, Mrs Hyslop?'

'No, not really. I just said that because I couldn't think of anything else he could be, all things considered.' She looked down and found that she was fumbling nervously with her crocheted bag. 'I don't understand any of it.'

'Of what?'

'The stuff that is scattered over his table. Maps, piles of newspaper cuttings and pieces of paper with strange things scrawled all over them. If Mr Kirchner had not seemed completely normal I might have doubted his sanity.'

'Have you tidied his room?' Jarrett asked.

'No, I wouldn't do that without his

155

permission, Superintendent. He hated it when any of his paperwork was moved.'

'Then I must ask you not to touch anything until we have examined the place.' Jarrett then turned to Tommy Quinn. It would have been entirely improper to put the lady through the trauma of making a formal identification, yet confirmation was required. His instructions were cryptic, but exactly what Quinn was expecting. 'See Dr Hamilton, Sergeant. Take young Chapman with you and get a couple of half plate portraitures. In life. Then meet me at Mrs Hyslop's house, 94 Benton Mews. Get PC Jamieson to take you and try to be as quick as possible.'

Tommy Quinn nodded and immediately departed.

⋆ ⋆ ⋆

When Charlie Grant returned to headquarters, along with DCs Williamson and Russell and a stunned-looking Wesley Bain, Davie Black informed him that the rest of the department was out and about. There had been a breakthrough, although exactly what it was he couldn't say because no one, he pointed out huffily, ever told him anything.

But Charlie understood and cursed once under his breath as he escorted Bain to the

156

interrogation room. More than ever he was convinced that he had drawn the short straw and was stuck with a boring little case of rogues falling out, while the boss and Tommy Quinn had landed a nice gory mystery they could really get their teeth into — figuratively speaking, of course.

Inspector Grant took his place across the table from the extremely uncomfortable Wesley Bain. He then laid the gun and bullet mould between them and sat back to consider the stall keeper.

It was Bain who broke the silence.

'I've never seen them before, Inspector,' he said, his voice wavering. 'Honestly, I don't know how they got there.'

'Perhaps they were under the scrap lead because that's where you hid them,' Charlie observed. 'It is the most obvious answer, after all.'

'Obvious to you, maybe, but not to me. Somebody is out — '

'To make sure you carry the can for their crime?'

'That's what I was going to say.'

'Naturally. That's what they all say. I had a gentleman recently who swore that several stolen wallets had been slipped into his coat pocket by a complete stranger.'

'But you didn't believe him?'

'On the contrary, I had already decided that he was telling the truth. That's what dips do, you see. If they think they're going to be searched they off-load their ill-gotten items onto whoever is nearby. If you can pick a pocket you can also fill one.'

Bain blinked, confused.

'Are you saying you believe that sort of thing happened to me?'

'I believe it's possible, Mr Bain. That is why you haven't been charged. Theoretically, you are at liberty to walk out of here and I can't stop you.'

'Theoretically?'

'Exactly. If you try it I'll hold you on suspicion, because if you are wholly innocent you will want to help me all you can.'

'I will, Inspector. I have already supplied you with information and I'll continue to do so if it will get me off this hook.'

'Good. That's what I like to hear,' Charlie Grant said. 'Now all we have to determine is who dislikes you enough to have you hang for a crime he committed. Perhaps you would like to tell me everything you know about the deceased, Gilbert Hayes.'

Bain gave this some thought and was clearly trying to decide where to begin.

'Well,' he said at length, 'I joined the fair in the Midlands just over three years ago. Hayes and most of the others you spoke to were already part of it.'

'Did you come from another fair?'

'No, the army. Seventeen years in the 101st Grenadiers, so I know about guns and casting bullets. In fact, it's all I know.'

Charlie then asked, 'How quickly can you get through a cask full of broken lead?'

'Not very quickly. I sort through the day's fired bullets and recast the distorted ones. Any that go into the wooden back board are usually good enough to use again.'

'I only mentioned it,' the inspector said, 'because it's my guess that whoever hid these items in there wanted us to find them, not you.'

'I see. Well, it would probably be months before I used up the scrap. In fact, I'm not buying in any pieces at the moment.'

Grant pondered this briefly.

'Who wants to see you hang, Mr Bain?' he asked.

'I've never been particularly cosy with any of them,' Bain admitted, 'but I didn't know I was that unpopular.'

'Any recent arguments?'

'None. All I can think of, Inspector, is that they took it badly when I supplied you with names to match the initials. Even then they couldn't have known for sure that it was me, unless you told them, of course.'

'I never reveal my sources.'

'Then they must have guessed.'

'Always assuming that the gun and mould were planted after I spoke to you. For all we can say these things might have been concealed under the lead immediately after the shooting. If that was the case they really were out to incriminate you. It is not impossible that your conviction was the real objective, with the death of Gilbert Hayes merely a bonus.'

'Surely not.' Wesley Bain stared at him in horror, his jaw loose and his fingers gripping the edge of the table until the white bones of his knuckles showed through the taut skin. 'If they hate me that much why didn't they just shoot me too.'

'It was only a possibility, nothing more.'

'Might it not just have been a convenient place to conceal the things?'

'Why not at the bottom of the river? The dredgers don't come up this far.' Charlie shook his head emphatically. 'No, Mr Bain, you were meant to take the drop for Gilbert Hayes's killing. I think we can set that fact aside now and concentrate on exactly who had access to your booth.'

Bain gave an expansive shrug.

'Almost anybody, I suppose,' he said, 'but it

would have to be after the fair closes for the evening, and even then they would have to be lightning quick.'

'Explain.'

'Well, the only time I leave my stall through the day is when I nip out for a pee, and that's just round the back of the tent. Your detective lad took quite a few minutes to empty the cask and just as long to put everything back again. I'm never away that long.'

'What about your dinner?'

'A boy brings me a pie and a mug of tea from Ma Harrison's Eating Booth.'

'After hours, then? What is there to stop someone gaining access to your booth at night?'

'A couple of watchmen with cudgels. Everybody contributes a few pennies a week to have their stalls protected.'

Grant made a mental note to talk to the sentinels.

'Tell me this, Mr Bain,' he said casually, 'how well do you get on with Boscombe himself?'

Bain looked decidedly concerned.

'We are not what you might call acquainted,' he answered. 'He tours the site every now and again and pretends to be interested in the rough end of the trade, but in truth we're just pig shit to him.'

'Have you ever got on his wrong side?'

'Not that I know of. I'm not that important, Inspector. I don't think Cyrus N. Boscombe would risk everything with a stunt like this.'

'All right, Mr Bain,' Charlie said, 'I have other enquiries to make, but in the meantime I'm going to have to detain you, partly because you are still the only suspect in this affair, and partly for your own safety.'

Wesley Bain looked decidedly dejected, but there was little he could do about it.

★ ★ ★

Jaguar Claw was on his knees, swaying, muttering and almost beside himself with shame. He had committed a dreadful sin and was begging forgiveness for an act that did not deserve to be forgiven. Although it was not his fault, the second heart was dead: sacrifices to the gods must still be throbbing when torn from the body and held aloft. It was still and clammy, like liver. The gods would not take kindly to this worst of all insults.

★ ★ ★

At 94 Benton Mews, Superintendent Henry Jarrett let his eyes drift over the comfortable little room that had been Johannes Kirchner's abode during his last five months on earth, and found it difficult not to compare it to his own dwelling at Elsie Maitland's guest-house. The only real difference, he concluded, stemmed from the natures of the occupants. Whereas he, Jarrett, tended to be precise and orderly, the late Mr Kirchner appeared to have had other priorities. Every available surface, including the floor area closest to the bed, was covered with documents, maps and densely-written notebooks.

Jarrett lifted one such book and found most of it indecipherable. Only the name was legible.

'Elisha Bradwell,' he said to the patient lady who had remained by the door for fear of disturbing anything. 'Does that mean anything to you, Mrs Hyslop?'

'Nothing at all, Superintendent,' she said honestly. 'Mr Kirchner never discussed his business affairs with me.'

'Did he have many visitors?'

'No, none.'

'Not one?'

'Not one, sir. I don't think Mr Kirchner was a particularly gregarious gentleman. Much too intense, if you know what I mean.'

'Single-minded?'

'And not in any way a jolly man. Quite

serious, in fact, but very sober and gracious with it.' Not once had this kindly lady enquired as to how or where Kirchner had met his fate, but now understandable curiosity, and more than a little concern, got the better of her and she asked, 'Was it murder, Superintendent?'

'I am not supposed to answer questions of that nature,' Jarrett said, 'especially if a positive identification has not been carried out.'

'But the ring . . . ?'

'There is always the possibility that the man in the mortuary is a thief who stole Mr Kirchner's ring before meeting his own untimely end, but that is extremely unlikely.'

'Who will formally identify the remains?'

'To be perfectly honest, Mrs Hyslop, we are hoping that you might, but since I have no intention of asking you to visit the mortuary Sergeant Quinn will be here soon with a photograph.'

The lady was clearly relieved by this and said, 'If you don't require me at the moment, Superintendent, I will leave you to it and go and make a pot of tea.'

Grateful for the opportunity to search the room thoroughly, Jarrett quickly drew the maps together, piled the various loose papers and notebooks on top of them and, after rolling the whole thing into a tube, secured it with a length of string he found in one of the drawers. A more thorough examination of this material would, he felt, be better carried out at headquarters.

Having set the maps and ephemera aside, Jarrett now found himself in a better position to approach things in the correct manner.

There was nothing whatsoever on top of the wardrobe and the sparse contents of this item of furniture suggested a man with absolutely no interest in fashion. Johannes Kirchner's clothes and footwear were strictly hard-wearing, functional and well made. The complete lack of colour and frippery supported Mrs Hyslop's description of the man as having been sober and single-minded.

There was a small portmanteau at the foot of the bed and after a swift, but thorough examination of the three drawers in the small corner cabinet, Jarrett turned his attention to this, which he felt might be the most profitable. Apart from the paperwork, there was nothing else in the room that held out the slightest promise.

At first he thought it was a Bible, then Jarrett realized that it was a black leather-bound, page-a-day Stamford diary. He flicked through it and saw that every page had a neat entry, sometimes full, sometimes partial, but never less than a dozen or so lines. The most recent addition was the previous day.

Jarrett returned the diary to the case, skimmed through a wad of newspaper cuttings held together with a bulldog clip, then laid them back inside, closed the container and placed it on the table beside the map roll for Quinn and Chapman to take with them and examine more fully.

★ ★ ★

Cyrus N. Boscombe was short, round and jovial. Everything, in fact, that Charlie Grant had not expected him to be.

He even drew open his caravan room door himself, so he either did not approve of keeping servants or he was as tight as Sadie Baker said he was. Yet miserliness and joviality did not somehow go hand in hand.

Charlie declined the offer of a drink, but was more than happy to accept a padded armchair and the opportunity to take the weight off his feet.

'A detective inspector?' Boscombe said, dropping into a matching chair on the other side of a long coffee table. 'What on earth am I supposed to have done?'

'Not you, sir. I am investigating the murder of Gilbert Hayes.'

Boscombe nodded grimly.

'Bad business, inspector,' he said. 'Didn't actually know the man myself. I believe he was one of the side-show people. There are so many, and they tend to come and go.'

'Precisely so, Mr Boscombe.'

'In what way can I help you?'

'Just by telling me how the whole thing operates. Someone killed Hayes and we are fairly sure it was not an outsider, so perhaps you can shed some light on the matter. For example, do you tour the show ground every day?'

'No, once when we arrive at a new place and again when we are packing up. My main interest is the menagerie. The animals are the main attraction, so their welfare is paramount.'

'May I ask how you built up the Boscombe Travelling Fair?'

'I didn't build it up, Inspector, I inherited it. My father was also Cyrus N. Boscombe, which meant that I didn't even have to paint out the name.'

Charlie Grant smiled at this.

'Just out of interest,' he said, 'what does the 'N' stand for?'

'Nothing.' Boscombe let out a large laugh for such a small man. 'I am sure you appreciate the joke, Inspector. N for Nothing.

It was my father's idea. He believed that all important men emphasized their middle initial. He did think about a hyphen, but somehow it didn't seem appropriate.'

Charlie nodded his complete agreement.

'Did you know he was a money-lender?' he asked suddenly. 'Gilbert Hayes, I mean.'

'I told you, I scarcely knew him beyond the occasional nod. As far as I can make out, he existed somewhere on the periphery of the showground. Such people could be up to anything.'

'So if you don't do the day-to-day managing of the fair, who does?'

'Horace Dinsley.'

'The man from the Ghost Tunnel?'

'Exactly. He has been with me for more than twenty years. Horace and his lads collect the site rents on my behalf and bring them to me here.' Boscombe jerked a thumb in the direction of an impregnable-looking safe in the far corner. 'I pay my employees and attend to council charges from it. The rest is profit.'

Charlie gave this some thought.

'If Gilbert Hayes had fallen foul of Dinsley,' he asked at length, 'what would they have done?'

'Well, they wouldn't have shot him dead behind the Ghost Tunnel,' Boscombe answered, grinning. 'Or anywhere else for that matter. Sorry, Inspector, but you will have to look further for your murderer. None of my people would be stupid enough to do a thing like that.'

'What about Wesley Bain? Is he stupid enough?'

'Hardly. They tell me that you have arrested the poor bugger, but quite frankly I can't see why. I doubt if he has the stuffing to kill anyone.'

'He was a regular soldier.'

'Who never saw action, I believe,' Boscombe said quickly. 'At least that's what Horace Dinsley tells me.'

Charlie's visit to Cyrus N. Boscombe had been pure routine — something Superintendent Jarrett would expect of him — but in truth he had expected it to be pointless. Little more than a courtesy call, in fact.

7

When Johannes Kirchner failed to appear at the Architectural Records Office, Elisha Bradwell's first assumption was that he had identified the property on which, or within which, the King's treasure boxes had been secreted. The idea that something untoward might have happened to the East African never occurred to him. On more than one occasion some indolent creature had tried to take a shortcut to riches by ambushing Kirchner or himself, just as claim-jumpers and poke-slitters used to do back in the days of the Gold Rush, but the two of them had seen too much and been on too many treasure trails not to have learnt how to look after themselves. No, it was generally accepted that they only had each other to worry about. Without actually saying as much, both Kirchner and Bradwell understood that this was the big one and that each man would be perfectly willing to put a bullet into the other rather than miss out. There was no second place in the hunt. It was all or dead.

Bradwell placed his Galilean binoculars on

the small table and leaned on the balcony rail, while he considered the situation and what his next move would be. Patience was something he had in abundance, ever since he was a child sitting on a slope beside the James River, dreaming about someday working on the big side-paddlers.

His childhood seemed a very long time ago now and a long way away. Some days he thought it had never really happened, and that he had always been a treasure hunter, endlessly reincarnated on the treadmill of life, but doomed never to find Eldorado, by any name.

Today was one such day; when Kirchner had left the Records Office the previous day he had been decidedly buoyant, even ebullient and Bradwell tried to reassure himself that he was imagining it and that he had no real cause for concern. Now, though, he knew that wasn't the case. His initial feeling had been true. Johannes Kirchner, rightly or wrongly, believed he was about to lay his hands on one of the great treasures of the world.

But one very serious problem remained and it applied to both of them equally. When the so-called Snake God story appeared in that local rag, the heart of Elisha Bradwell had come as close to stopping as it ever had done, and there was no doubt in his mind that Johannes Kirchner had experienced that same moment of absolute horror. By whatever means, the police now had the eight boxes and that meant they were lost forever as far as the searchers were concerned. Yet within a very short period of time a combination of reason and bribery demonstrated that this was not the case.

The police had one box, according to Bradwell's source, and this was more or less confirmed when Kirchner made his regular appearance at the Records Office. This he would not have done if all had been lost. Nor could the East African have been ignorant of this awkward development. He took all the papers, daily and weekly, and he had his own sources, yet it was clear that he still saw the game as winnable.

Elisha Bradwell turned abruptly, slid open the glazed doors and made directly for the narrow cupboard in the darkest corner of the room where his cased LeMat revolver had rested since his arrival. He unclipped the lid of the gun's box, raised it and almost reverentially removed the gun. Yet it was far from being a work of art. Rather, it was a short and nasty contraption of .44 calibre, with a second barrel underneath that was effectively a .65, 18-gauge shotgun. The range was poor, but up close it was fearsome.

It would be murder for gain. A capital offence in any country, anywhere, but the alternative would be to live on for God knew how many years knowing that Johannes Kirchner had won the day.

Then came an almost imperceptible and rather discreet knock on the main door of his apartment. Bradwell transferred the gun to his left hand and held it behind him as he drew open the door. A short, neatly-uniformed boy, who was scarcely more than a child, held out a silver tray on which lay a small blue envelope. Bradwell took the item and held it between his teeth while he fished out two bright pennies to reward the lad.

Alone again, he placed the LeMat on his fireside table and examined the envelope, noting that it had been posted in the city centre earlier that morning. He then broke the red wax seal and shook open the single sheet.

Elisha Bradwell Esq.,
If you desire beyond all things to learn the whereabouts of the grave goods of Pezelao, be at the corner of Ingram Street and Hanover Street around 4 p.m. this afternoon. If you have not put in an appearance by 5 p.m. I must assume that you are not sufficiently interested.

The letter contained neither the sender's name nor address, and might well be a hoax or a trap, but either way it could not be ignored.

Bradwell dug out his pocket watch, checked it against the mock-Ormolu clock on the mantelpiece: it was 3.21 p.m. Since there was nothing else for it, he put on his coat, made sure he had sufficient cab money, then briefly considered the pros and cons of taking the LeMat with him.

On balance, he decided that it would be best to take it.

★   ★   ★

Having returned to headquarters, Superintendent Henry Jarrett had no sooner settled down to attend to the afternoon mail than a young constable appeared at the door to announce that someone desired to speak with the chief immediately. To Jarrett's dismay the visitor turned out to be the Guatemalan Consul, Gideon Mallam.

'The Chief Constable is ill,' Jarrett said, once the unwelcome arrival had made himself comfortable on the other side of the large desk. 'Having said that, though he is no more in a position to hand over the finds than I. The matter is entirely out of our hands.'

'Indeed it is, Superintendent,' Mallam said smugly. 'I have been in telegraphic communication with the ambassador in the London Guatemalan embassy. He has intimated that he proposes to take the whole affair up with the Foreign Office.'

'Then I must repeat my original argument, Mr Mallam. The chest and all it contains are evidence in a murder case. No court in the land can order it to be handed over to a third party, however strong the claim.'

'I think you'll find it to be otherwise. Great Britain and Guatemala are involved in very complicated trade negotiations, involving coffee and timber on the one hand and a wide variety of British-made goods on the other. It is, after all, a mere four years since Guatemala was forced to cede to the Crown the land now known as British Honduras. As you can imagine diplomatic relations are strained and the current negotiations at a rather delicate stage.'

'Perhaps so,' Jarrett said, 'but that alters nothing. Unless the Procurator Fiscal decides not to prosecute the murder case, all things pertaining to it remain in the vaults.'

Mallam jumped abruptly to his feet, yet managed to keep his expression even and unrevealing.

'I think you are making a grave mistake,

Superintendent,' he said. 'Indeed, you may even be putting yourself in jeopardy. I really don't think you know what you are dealing with.'

'Are you threatening me, Mr Mallam?'

'No, not I. But there are those who will stop at nothing to get their hands on those artefacts.'

No sooner had Gideon Mallam departed than young Walter Chapman appeared, still somewhat reserved and conscious of the temporary nature of his position.

'Excuse me, sir,' he said. 'Sergeant Quinn would like to know if you would care to join us in the map room. If you are not too busy, that is.'

Tommy Quinn had been hunched over the largest of Kirchner's maps, but he and acting-DC Chapman stood erect when Jarrett arrived.

'I think we know what we are dealing with, Superintendent,' Quinn stated. 'It fits in exactly with Professor Greenaway's account of the legends.

'Johannes Kirchner was obviously a professional treasure seeker on the trail of the eight boxes mentioned by Greenaway in both the *Nuestra Señora de Cartagena* and the Jacobite legends. And he wasn't the only one. There are several references to one Elisha

Bradwell in Kirchner's diary among other scribbles. Judging by the change of tone, Kirchner and Bradwell had been in league on a number of occasions, but in competition on others. Lately they were decidedly at odds.'

'Which suggests that this Bradwell individual should be at the top of our list of suspects for the Kirchner murder,' Jarrett added.

'I would agree with you there, sir, but only if the strain of it all has caused Bradwell to lose his reason. I mean, two normal men at loggerheads with each other might resort to guns, knives or blunt instruments, but what happened to Johannes Kirchner was not the work of a sane man.'

'Or, that may merely be the conclusion the murderer intends us to draw.'

'Yes, that is certainly a possibility. Dr Hamilton is of the opinion that it would require only slight anatomical knowledge and a familiarity with the way the high priests carried out the sacrifices.'

'Plus a strong stomach,' Jarrett observed.

'A butcher, perhaps,' young Chapman ventured, then looked suddenly abashed as though anticipating admonition for talking out of turn.

But he needn't have worried.

'Good suggestion, Constable,' Henry Jarrett said, 'but in this case I would suggest that a hunter might be closer to the truth. I don't know the first thing about these treasure seekers, but I should imagine that they would have to be self-sufficient, especially if they find themselves in some God-awful part of the world.'

Tommy Quinn was thoughtful for a few moments.

'I still can't quite see why Bradwell would go to all that trouble, unless of course there are others who need to be frightened off.'

'I shouldn't imagine that a keen treasure hunter would be scared off by a gruesome stunt, because if we are perfectly honest that is exactly what this is. Dr Hamilton is of the opinion that it was probably a consequence of McGovern's irresponsible article in the *Advertiser*, and I am inclined to agree.'

'But what if there are others, less dedicated than either Kirchner or Bradwell, people who are perhaps just in the way,' Quinn said. 'If Bradwell wanted to remove his greatest rival, while at the same time send the opportunists running for the hills, I can think of no more effective way of doing it.'

'But that would rely entirely on the nature of Kirchner's fate being made public.'

'Exactly, Superintendent,' DS Quinn said,

grinning, 'but we denied him that by letting McGovern think it was just another boozy stabbing. Not headline material.'

'And we must keep it that way.' Jarrett glanced at Acting Detective Constable Chapman, but it was clear that the boy did not require reminding on that score. 'What we have to do now is locate Elisha Bradwell. Ideas, gentlemen?'

Not willing to forfeit such an invitation from a senior officer, Walter Chapman said, 'We could place a notice in the *Advertiser*, Superintendent. 'Would Elisha Bradwell please get in touch with the Detective Department at Glasgow Central as soon as possible'.'

'Do you really think he will?' Tommy Quinn asked, amused.

'No, Sergeant, but I think anyone living in close proximity almost certainly would. Just in case there is a reward.'

'You have a refreshingly poor opinion of your fellow man,' Jarrett said. 'But in truth the bird will take flight as soon as the notice appears. I'm afraid there would be nothing in the nest when we got there.'

'Precisely, Superintendent, but at least we will have flushed him out.'

Henry Jarrett considered this, then turned to Quinn.

'What do you think, Sergeant? If we have a

presence at the railway stations, shipping offices and coach companies we could scoop him up.'

'If we knew what he looked like or was foolish enough to be in possession of anything that might identify him.'

'True, but can you improve on young Chapman's suggestion?'

'Well, I can only say what I would do in Elisha Bradwell's position.'

'And that is?'

'I would find fresh digs under a different name, and I would do it immediately. After all, the thing he wants most is right here somewhere, so he isn't likely to run off and leave it for someone else to find.'

'What if he isn't in digs? If he has a property it wouldn't be possible for him to change addresses.'

'Is that likely, sir? I think we can assume that he has come to Glasgow from elsewhere, just as Kirchner did. Such people would not buy bricks and mortar. They are always going to be ready to move on at a moment's notice.'

Jarrett nodded.

'Point taken, Sergeant,' he said. 'Now, why don't you improve on Chapman's suggestion?'

Tommy Quinn shrugged lightly.

'I don't think I can,' he admitted. 'It is

probably as good an idea as any. I was merely pointing out where it could go wrong.'

'Then let us do it,' Jarrett instructed. 'Constable, I want you to draft the notice for my approval, then get round to the *Advertiser* office right away and get them to insert it.'

'Will the editor accept it from me, Superintendent?'

'McGovern? Yes, he'll accept it all right, and with a bit of luck he won't attach any great importance to it. No disrespect, lad, but I am banking on his not realizing its significance since it is being entrusted to an officer of such a lowly rank.'

Far from taking offence, Walter Chapman gave a smart salute, fished out his notebook and pencil, and set about wording the notice for Henry Jarrett to peruse and approve.

* * *

Larry Reed and Jem Weaver had been, and probably still were, bare-knuckle boxers of the old-time variety. Not in the same class as the legendary Tom Cribb, but still perfectly capable of reducing Charlie Grant to a bloody pulp if the inclination took them. The shiny brass badge, however, was a great equalizer.

'It was just a joke, sir,' Jem offered. They

were in a makeshift hut that was assembled and dismantled every time the fair moved on, so that now the timber walls were riddled by hundreds of large nail holes and the tarp roof no longer kept out the rain. 'We didn't know it would get Mr Bain arrested.'

'Tell me exactly what happened,' Charlie said.

'We got half a crown each, that's what happened,' Larry Reed put in, then stuck his clay pipe back between brown teeth.

'For?'

'Turning a blind eye,' Jem continued. 'The idea was that we were to take ourselves off for a quarter of an hour so's that they could play a trick on Wesley Bain.'

'And who exactly are 'they'?'

'Don't know. It mightn't have been 'they'. It could have been a him or a her.'

'Who gave you the five bob?'

'Billy Roake. He's the runaway who does all the running and fetching around here.'

'So who gave him the money?'

'You'll have to ask him that, Inspector, but he'll take a bit of catching. Unless you wait until the fair closes for the day. Then you'll find him under the lion house. Says he feels safe in there.' Jem waited until Charlie Grant was ducking under the low doorway to take his leave, then added, 'You won't say anything to Mr Boscombe about this, will you, sir? We'd get our marching orders right away.'

Charlie nodded.

'If you've been straight with me,' he said, 'there's no reason why he should ever hear of it.'

* * *

In the not too distant future, the whole district known as Grahamston was going to be demolished to make way for a large railway station. Every proprietor and shopkeeper had received official notice of this and all were hanging on in anticipation of a substantial amount of compensation. Rufus Fogarty was no exception. It filled his waking and sleeping dreams, and nothing cheered him more than the thought of returning to his homeland a successful and wealthy man.

For the moment, however, Fogarty's Hotel was little more than an infested flea pit at the far end of Green Bottle Lane. Tarts or two men might rent a curtained cubicle for a few pennies an hour, and the truly desperate had even been known to sleep there. But not many. It was the ideal place in which to wake up dead. Although in truth that had never actually happened.

Until now.

Rufus Fogarty was a man almost entirely devoid of curiosity, but when two men went up to the second floor and only one came back down again even he was inclined to wonder why.

Slowly, because he wasn't as agile as he once was, and because he had no wish to find himself in the kind of awkward situation even the blarney couldn't get him out of, he climbed the rickety stairs to the narrow passage, but even with a few treads still to go he could see that something was terribly wrong.

At first it looked as though a length of curtain had been tugged from its rings and was trailing on the uneven timber floor. Then, to his utter horror, Fogarty realized that it was a thick trail of blood. Despite telling himself again and again that this was not a sensible thing to do, he found himself moving forward, arm outstretched, until his thin fingers reached the coarse drapes.

* * *

Billy Roake could have been scarcely more than ten or so years of age, but he had the beginnings of a leathery, weatherbeaten face and a swagger that would have done justice to a ganger.

When Inspector Grant's fingers bit into his shoulder the boy came within a hair's breadth of cursing the stranger's antecedents, but the badge saved him from a thick ear.

'You're not easy to trap, young fellow,' the inspector said truthfully. For the previous forty-five minutes he had been enquiring as to where the boy might be found, and had finally come to the conclusion that he was doomed to be just a minute behind him for all eternity. 'I want to talk to you.'

Billy frowned and tugged his shoulder several times until he released it from Charlie Grant's hold.

'What about?' he demanded.

'We could start with bribing Larry Reed and Jem Weaver. That makes you an accessory to the burgling of Wesley Bain's stall.'

Far from being frightened by this, Billy said, 'Burgling my arse. It was a caper.'

'Don't you like Mr Bain?'

'He's all right, but it wasn't me that was playing the joke. I'm just the gopher.'

'Who was it?' Charlie produced a sixpenny piece from his waistcoat pocket, but didn't hand it over just yet. 'Who gave you the five shillings for Reed and Weaver?'

There was no doubt that Billy wanted the coin, and it no doubt occurred to him that a lie would enable him to get his hands on it, but at the same time this policeman was not the sort of man who could take that sort of thing in good part.

'I don't know who it was,' the boy admitted after a brief inner struggle.

'Do you think I'm going to fall for that?' Charlie asked. 'You must know everyone in the travelling fair. It isn't possible for someone to approach you without being recognized.'

'It is if their voice is muffled.'

'Nonsense. You've either been watching too many bad plays or you've been wasting your money on Penny Dreadfuls, but I'll tell you this, young fellow, you'll not fool me with a yarn like that.'

'It's no yarn, mister. I was in my place under the lion house when he knelt down and told me what he wanted me to do, but I don't know who he was because he had a scarf over his mouth. He threw the two half-crowns and a threepenny down beside me and hurried away.'

'Just supposing I believe you,' Charlie said cautiously, 'how do you know it was a man?'

Billy gave thought to this.

'I'm pretty sure it was a man,' he offered, 'but it might have been a woman with a deep voice, or making out she had.'

'What exactly did this person tell you about

the so-called caper he was going to play on Mr Bain?'

'That's all he said, sir. He didn't say anything else.'

'But you must have guessed at what it was all about.'

'I suppose so.' Again, the boy fell silent, then added, 'I reckoned he was going to sort of get his own back for Wesley Bain talking freely to you, sir.'

Inspector Grant found himself nodding in agreement with this.

'That would make sense, lad,' he said, surrendering the bright sixpence and watching the boy tuck it away in a small pigskin purse. 'Do you know anything else that might interest me?'

The boy shrugged lightly.

'I've told you all I know, mister,' he mumbled.

'Perhaps, perhaps not. It's my guess that not much goes by you. Don't expect me to believe that you weren't curious, Billy.'

'Well, maybe a little.'

'Curious enough to sneak out at night and watch the goings on?'

For the first time the boy's eyes widened and he reflected fear.

'Not me,' he whispered. 'I know when to mind my own business.'

Then he was gone, darting through the forest of people and jumping the guy ropes with all the agility of the inhabitants of the monkey house.

8

The man on the narrow bunk was naked and dead. The thin mattress on which he lay was smeared with blood rather than saturated. Yet, as in the case of Johannes Kirchner, a hideous gash extended from his stomach to his thorax.

'Watch your feet, Superintendent,' Dr Hamilton said over his shoulder. 'You have at least one decent bloody foot-print that might help.'

'A naked foot-print,' Henry Jarrett observed. 'Could the killer also have been in the same natural state, do you think, Doctor?'

'Possibly, but there was no sign of sexual activity in Kirchner's case and I don't expect to find any here.'

'What about the victim's clothes and other possessions?'

'Gone, I'm afraid. I am not trying to do your job for you, Superintendent, but the owner of this grim establishment volunteered the information that one of the men was carrying a large bag when he arrived and took it with him when he left. It's my guess that this was entirely premeditated and that everything was removed to make it difficult to identify this chap.'

'The killer left Kirchner's ring, knowing full well that it would eventually put a name to him.'

'Perhaps, but so far I have found nothing comparable. No jewellery or tattoos, but we do have a couple of healed scars which someone might recognize. One in particular is definitely a bullet wound.'

'And the cause of death?' Jarrett asked.

'More or less as before.' Even though there was no one else on the top landing Dr Hamilton lowered his voice until it was barely more than a whisper. 'But this time at least you have a description of the killer.'

'We shall see.' Jarrett's thoughts at that moment were more on how Sergeant Tommy Quinn was getting on with his interviewing of Rufus Fogarty downstairs at the reception desk. And there was also young Walter Chapman, who had been left back at headquarters studying Johannes Kirchner's diary and jottings. Jarrett was now experiencing a rapidly growing sense of urgency, rather like a train driver heading at top speed for the buffers and unable to do anything about it; this was not the way he wanted his career to end. 'What is your reading of the corpse, Doctor?'

'Well, the bullet hole apart, there are also several scars that could have been caused by knives or the like. Also, the hands are not those of a clerk or professional person. This man has been used to hard work, though not recently, and it is my guess that he had his share of trouble.'

'That's the impression I get.' Jarrett shook his head grimly. 'I have a dreadful feeling that I have made a serious mistake.'

'In what way?'

'For absolutely no good reason, other than the fact that his name cropped up in several of Kirchner's scribblings, I'd assumed that Elisha Bradwell murdered the East African. Now I am beginning to think that this may be Bradwell. If so, I have no suspects at all.'

'You have an eye-witness.'

'Fogarty? Unless I am a poor judge of character, Sergeant Quinn is unlikely to get anything useful from him. The man is a nervous wreck.'

'Hardly surprising, Superintendent. He may have seen a thing or two in his life, but I'll wager he never saw anything like this before.'

Henry Jarrett looked down at the blood on the floor.

'I would have expected more of a mess,' he admitted. 'Does it look right to you, Doctor?'

'Perfectly right,' Hamilton said, 'for a man who was already dead when he was cut open. I think we'll discover that he has a thin skull and that the blow killed him instantly. He probably went through his whole life without knowing that he could have died at any moment from a minor fall or an impact with a low branch.'

★ ★ ★

Charlie Grant was still fairly sure that the identity of Gilbert Hayes's killer was to be found among the sets of initials in the money-lender's book, but it was a theory that was quickly losing its appeal. He had just wasted two hours talking to the same people he had spoken to before, without learning anything new, and certainly not the identity of the mysterious individual who gave Billy Roake his instructions. The only thing the whole experience taught him was that if they were all colluding, they demonstrated astonishing loyalty to one of their number, or else something very powerful indeed was keeping them unified and unable to speak freely.

From the very start one aspect of this crime had made little or no sense. And the more he thought about it the more irrational it seemed. Any normal villain would have forced Gilbert Hayes to produce his cash-box at gunpoint, then either killed him, or not. But here the police were being asked to believe that the killer lured Hayes to a quiet spot behind Horace Dinsley's Ghost Tunnel, murdered him, then ransacked the victim's van in the hope of finding the money. Charlie Grant was rapidly finding it very difficult to accept that the murderer could carefully select a suitable weapon, use just the right amount of black powder to kill Hayes without causing an explosion that could be heard over the hammering and shouting of the labourers, then gain access to the shooting booth after hours to secret the weapon where it would incriminate Wesley Bain, all without having the first idea where Hayes's savings were concealed.

Sadie Baker was still leaning on her counter next to the deserted archery stall and still shuffling the cards.

'I've told you everything I know, Inspector,' she stated. 'To be perfectly honest, I don't think there was much to him. He was a bit of a dry stick. As I said already, I didn't have much time for him myself.'

'But you must have heard something,' Charlie encouraged. 'Tales get bandied about all the time, especially in a tight-knit community like this.'

'What sort of tales, Inspector?'

'Just about anything. Apart from being a money-lender, was he involved in other things?'

'What other things?'

'Well, let us say I am finding it a bit difficult to believe that Hayes was murdered for his savings.'

Sadie shrugged.

'Why not? He must have been worth a few bob, the skinflint. Apart from the van he didn't lash out on very much.'

'That's not quite what I meant,' Charlie admitted. 'I don't want to go too deeply into the details, but the circumstances of his death do not add up.'

Sadie looked pensive.

'I can't imagine any other reason for killing him,' she said at length. 'I suppose his customers didn't take to him too much, and it stands to reason that he would have salted a bit away, but that could be said of a lot of people. I can think offhand of a couple of dozen showmen around here who have gathered together bigger nest eggs, but nobody has killed them or rifled their vans.'

'What about outsiders?'

'How do you mean?'

'Did you ever see Gilbert Hayes with anyone who wasn't from the show?'

Sadie shook her head.

'Only customers,' she said. 'Anyway, I don't think there's much profit in looking beyond the fair. For my money Hayes's killer is right here, so yours truly is taking more care than usual. I always padlock my van when I'm here and I've had an extra bolt fitted for night-time.'

* * *

For once, Superintendent Henry Jarrett had no complaint about the *Advertiser*'s treatment of young Walter Chapman's request for a public notice that Elisha Bradwell should put in an appearance at headquarters. Jake McGovern clearly had not linked the appeal to his own outrageous article on the jade mask, and as a result had printed it just as it was laid out. At best, Bradwell was still alive and would comply with the suggestion of the police that he show up and be counted. On the other hand, it might result in the identification of the corpse in Fogarty's hotel, particularly if anyone had noted the absence of Bradwell within the last few hours. But whatever the outcome, Jarrett could see no real harm in complying with the lad's suggestion.

He handed the folded paper to Tommy

Quinn and seated himself behind the large desk.

'Chapman?' he asked.

'Still going through Kirchner's accumulated stuff,' Sergeant Quinn said, smiling. 'The boy has the patience of Job. There are hundreds of jottings and God knows what to be gone though.'

'I think we should let him get on with it. He isn't ready yet for murders of this nature. And as far as we are concerned, we can only hope that there is another Mrs Hyslop out there somewhere who has misplaced an Elisha Bradwell.'

Tommy Quinn put the paper to one side.

'So you think the corpse in the mortuary really is Bradwell, Superintendent?'

'Without having the slightest reason for it, yes, I do. I would very much like to think I am wrong, Sergeant, because my only other suspect is in a better position to kick up a storm and make the investigation very difficult indeed.'

'Forgive me, sir,' Quinn said, a slight smile on his lips, 'but I wasn't aware of having any other suspects apart from Bradwell.'

'What about Gideon Mallam?' Jarrett suggested.

Now Quinn's smile turned into a broad grin.

'The Guatemalan consul, Superintendent?'

'I'm not joking, Sergeant Quinn. Mallam is a thoroughly avaricious man. It is in his face, and reading faces is something I am pretty good at. You may take it from me that all his talk about claiming the tomb goods for the country he represents is just so much eyewash. Mallam wants it for Mallam. It would be bad enough for such a man to know that we had one of the boxes, but a great deal worse to learn that professional treasure-hunters were on the trail of all the rest of it.'

'You honestly think him capable of anything as vicious as these killings?'

'Why not? He may well be insane, or he may just be cold-blooded and very clever. He might not be planning to get caught, but it would be a good idea to feign madness at this stage so that he would at least escape the gallows.'

'I suppose it has been done before.'

'On numerous occasions, I can assure you.' Jarrett paused, then, 'I want you to investigate our Mr Mallam, but proceed with caution and don't involve any of the DCs. I would rather he weren't warned of our interest.'

'Do you think he will claim diplomatic immunity, Superintendent?'

'Not possible, fortunately. Mallam has already admitted in a roundabout way that he is still a British citizen operating as a consul for a foreign nation. He cannot claim diplomatic immunity, but he could make things warm for us at a political level by alleging victimization.'

'In that case, sir,' Tommy Quinn said, 'should we not wait until the most recent victim has been positively identified as Bradwell?'

'No, I don't think so, Sergeant. Even if Mallam is not a killer I want to know more about him than I do. And while you are at it, find out all you can about Guatemala.'

★ ★ ★

The girl could have been anything from fifteen to twenty. She was small, slim and free of tart's rouge on her cheeks or colour on her lips. When she spoke it was in low, reverential whispers, and she averted her eyes because everyone else was her superior.

'Are you sure?' Davie Black asked when she had told him about the missing Mr Bradwell.

'Very sure, sir,' she said softly, 'but the manager mustn't know I told you. The hotel is trying to keep it quiet for as long as possible.'

'Then why are you risking your position by

reporting it, my girl?'

'Because it's my duty, of course.' Then, after a few moments added, 'Is there a reward?'

'Can't say. It was the tecs who put this piece in the paper, so only they can answer that. Perhaps you should speak to the great man himself. But be on your best behaviour, girl, because he's so far above the likes of you that it would be like looking at the sun.' When he saw the girl's eyes widen in terror, Davie quickly continued with, 'For God's sake I'm only kidding. Have you no sense of humour?'

'We're not allowed anything like that,' she said.

'Really? It must be all high jinks and jollification, that place.'

'It's better than being on the streets, sir.'

'Yes, I suppose it is.' Davie Black waved one of the young PCs over. 'Take this young lady to see Superintendent Jarrett.'

'What if he's busy, Sergeant?'

'Then you'll get it in the neck, won't you? Now, on you go and get back as quickly as you can.'

*　*　*

Guilt was getting the better of Lizzie Gill to the extent that she made her mind up to come clean and put an end to Jeannie Craig's sufferings. The poor girl was near to working herself to death, she thought, and I alone have the power to put an end to it by telling her about the Largs letter.

That, then, was Lizzie's frame of mind when Jeannie arrived back in the kitchen and began on her share of the vegetables. Even here she demonstrated her new whirlwind self and was clearly determined to prove that she and she alone was indispensable.

'I've got something to tell you, Jeannie,' Lizzie said, hesitatingly. 'I don't know if you'll think it's good or bad news, all things considered.'

Jeannie frowned at her, but there was not the slightest break in her frantic scraping.

'Go on, then, but make it quick. I've got a lot of things to do yet.'

'Very well.' Lizzie paused briefly, before adding, 'It's all for nothing. They're not going to go to Largs. Honest. Mr Jarrett threw away the letter and told the house-agent that they weren't interested any more.'

Jeannie stared hard at her and the knife froze in mid-carrot.

'I can't believe that you would stoop to such a dirty trick, Lizzie Gill,' she hissed. 'Just imagine making up a story like that to make me stop my chores. You must be very desperate to be the chosen one if you are willing to come out with the first pack of lies that occurs to you.'

'But it's true.'

'Rubbish! I've been watching them and believe me it's all coming to a head. I heard him calling her 'Elsie' in private and she was calling him 'Henry', but when anyone else is around it's Mrs Maitland and Superintendent. Just last night he almost said 'Elsie' in the front hall, but she put a finger to her mouth and stopped him in time. Most people wouldn't have noticed, but I'm not most people.'

'What does that prove?'

'Everything. Don't be so dense, Miss Gill. It's all there for the reading.'

'Well, perhaps I'm not as canny as you are,' Lizzie said, suddenly wishing that she had not confessed to this unappreciative creature. 'You can believe what you want and I'll believe what I want.'

'Agreed. We know where we stand. And next time you dream up some desperate scheme to get ahead of me just keep it to yourself.'

★ ★ ★

'Moira Pearce,' the girl said in answer to Jarrett's question. 'Maid, Victoria Hotel.'

'And you claim to have information about Elisha Bradwell?'

'I have, but as I told the other policeman I'd rather the manager didn't know I was here. I wouldn't have been, but this is my afternoon off so nobody knows.'

'I think I can assure you that no one will, Miss Pearce. Whatever you have to tell us will be held in confidence.' Henry Jarrett clasped his hands on the blotter and hoped he was presenting a benign face. 'Now, take your time and remember that every little detail may be important.'

'Actually,' the girl whispered, 'I was hoping there might be a reward, sir.'

'If your information turns out to be useful, you will be recompensed for your time and trouble. We keep a small fund for that very purpose.'

'Well, sir,' she said, brighter now, 'Mr Bradwell arrived at the hotel about two weeks ago. He seemed to stick out from the other guests, him being an American or something like that. Also, his luggage seemed a bit odd. Usually, guests have cases and chests, especially if they are from overseas, but he didn't have much in the way of luggage. It was mainly tubes and other odd things.'

'Map tubes,' Jarrett suggested.

'Yes, sir. Whenever I went in to perform my

duties there was always at least one map spread out. I was never supposed to touch anything like that, so I had to explain to the supervisor that I couldn't do the room to expected standards.'

Jarrett nodded. The similarity between the girl's description of Bradwell's preferred environment and Johannes Kirchner's room at Mrs Hyslop's boarding house was remarkable.

'Before you proceed, Miss Pearce, what made you think that Elisha Bradwell was missing and not merely off on a jaunt?'

'The fact that he never went off on a jaunt, as you put it, sir. He wasn't like other visitors, you see. He wasn't the tourist sort, if you see what I mean.'

'But surely he was in the habit of going out and about?'

'Sometimes, sir, but not often. He spent much of his time on the balcony. I saw him quite often just sitting there with his binoculars, peering at things.'

'Do you know what he was watching?'

'No, sir. People, I think, more than buildings. He seemed to be following a person who was moving, rather than staring at an object.'

'That is most interesting Miss Pearce. You are a very observant young lady. Perhaps you could tell me whether there was a pattern to his forays from the hotel.'

'Well, sir, he did occasionally go out for a short time in the forenoons, and sometimes quite recently he would leave the hotel in the evening, but I couldn't say when he got back because I was off-duty by then. Anyway, the hotel is open day and night. It isn't like a landlady who says when you have to be in if you don't want to spend the night on the doorstep.'

This caused Jarrett to smile. It was clear that the girl had been in private service.

'So you have no way of knowing where he went to in the evenings?' he asked.

'No, sir.' She looked slightly embarrassed. 'I just thought it might be the sort of thing that men do.'

'You mean ladies of the night.'

'That kind of thing, sir, yes.'

'Do you have any reason to suppose it was that?'

'Only the fact that he suggested matters to me not long after he arrived, sir. I suppose it's quite commonplace in hotels around the world, so he took it for granted.'

'What did he say?'

'He asked me how much I earned and told me he would leave some money on the mantelpiece for me if I did him a special favour. Naturally, I said I wasn't like that.'

'What did he do then?'

'He just laughed and said that I would have to whistle another tune if I ever wanted to land a toff. But there was never another mention after that.'

'Did you report it to the manager?'

'Not me, sir. He would have sided with the guest and probably accused me of leading him on. That's the quickest way to get shown the door, sir.'

After a few moments Jarrett asked, 'Did anyone ever visit Bradwell?'

'Not that I know of, but I wasn't always on his floor.' After a few seconds she said, 'I dare say you'll go to the room and examine his belongings. You won't tell anybody about this talk?'

'I have already told you, Miss Pearce. Nobody will find out where we got our information from.'

★ ★ ★

It was a somewhat disgruntled Charlie Grant who arrived back at headquarters, just in time to find Superintendent Jarrett preparing to depart for the Victoria Hotel. After some discussion, it was agreed that the inspector was wasting his time on the fairground killing and, until some other development occurred he would be better working with his colleagues. Anyway, Grant had left William-son and Russell on-site to speak to literally every person who had anything to do with the shows, so it wasn't as though that enquiry was an entirely dead duck.

Two uniformed constables had been sent on ahead to make sure that Elisha Bradwell's room was not touched, and a message had been left for Tommy Quinn, instructing him to make his way there as soon as possible. In the event, police driver Jamieson spotted the detective sergeant at the corner of Hope Street and Bothwell Street.

'That saved a bit of time,' Tommy Quinn said cheerfully as he climbed into the wagonette. 'I got what we needed on Guatemala from the Chamber of Commerce. Do you wish it now, Superintendent.'

Jarrett quickly apprised Inspector Grant of his suspicions about Consul Mallam, then said, 'Please proceed, Sergeant.'

'Well, sir, it would appear that Rafael Carrera, the present dictator, was an illiterate swineherd and robber who seized power in a popular uprising over heavy taxes and a cholera epidemic. He has been in power now since 1844, and in 1854 declared himself President for Life. The relations with Britain are not good. He foolishly believed us when we told him we would build him a road across the country in exchange for part of his territory. We got what we now call British Honduras, but he didn't get his road. He is currently claiming compensation. Also, earlier this year he declared war on President Barrios of El Salvador.'

'Which reinforces our opinion that Mallam wants the treasure for himself,' Jarrett said. 'I can't imagine him being willing to hand it over to this character.'

'Under no circumstances, sir,' Tommy Quinn agreed.

'So it follows on that his claim to have been in touch with their ambassador in London is an outright lie.'

'Unless they planned to share the proceeds,' Charlie Grant put in.

'Possible, but why even tell him about it in the first place? No, Inspector, I think Mallam is one hundred per cent out for himself and that he will stop at nothing to reach his objective.'

Tommy Quinn thought for a few moments, then, 'If he did try to scare off Bradwell by murdering Kirchner in such a fashion, who was he trying to dissuade by repeating the whole gory performance with Bradwell — us?'

'I hardly think so,' Charlie Grant offered. 'Crazy or sane, nobody expects to scare the police into giving up an investigation. No, the only thing I can think of is that there's another of these treasure-hunters we haven't heard about so far.'

Jarrett nodded in agreement.

'That's a possibility,' he said. 'Perhaps there will be something in Bradwell's belongings that will shed some light on it.'

★ ★ ★

Victor Middleton was a burly walrus of a man, who was plainly in the habit of ordering minions about and getting his own way in every respect. So it came as something of a shock to discover that the detectives were also used to being obeyed.

'It isn't open to debate,' Henry Jarrett told him flatly. 'My men are already guarding the room and now I want access to it. I sincerely hope that nothing has been rearranged or removed.'

The heavy man attempted to outstare the superintendent, but after a few moments caved in and snapped his fingers in the general direction of the reception clerk.

'The key to 205,' he snapped.

The unfortunate man turned, found the

hook to be empty, then said in a croaky manner, 'It hasn't been surrendered.'

'What are you talking about, Coulter? The key must be handed in when a guest leaves the premises. That's the rule.'

'I know, Mr Middleton, but on this occasion the gentleman appears to have taken it with him.'

'Then send a boy to get the maid's key, and tell him to take it straight to the room.' Middleton turned again to Jarrett. 'May I ask who informed the police of Mr Bradwell's absence? And for that matter why should the disappearance of a grown man for such a short period interest you?'

'I'm afraid I can't answer either of those questions, sir. Now, if you would lead the way we can get on with our investigations.'

As expected, Elisha Bradwell's room bore a startling resemblance to the one hastily vacated by Johannes Kirchner. They were, after all, in the same line of business and apparently shared a similar temperament. Neither was obsessed with maintaining a tidy environment.

Tommy Quinn unrolled a large linen-backed map.

'Most recent Ordnance Survey of Glasgow, sir,' he said. 'Same one as Kirchner had and with similar markings.'

Even though Charlie Grant had come late to this case and was still smarting over having wasted so much time achieving nothing at the fairground, he rapidly soaked up everything there was to know about the sacrificial killings, as Jarrett termed them.

'What about a positive identification, Superintendent?' he asked when Middleton had departed to persecute his staff.

'Sergeant Quinn and young Chapman will pay a call on Dr Hamilton later and capture the corpse's likeness on a collodion plate. Trouble is, Inspector, we can't ask the hotel maid to identify him or that overbearing manager will see her on the pavement.'

'The desk clerk could put a name to him, surely?'

'That won't be necessary.' Tommy Quinn was grinning broadly now and holding up a quarter plate studio portrait for them both to see. It was one of several in a leather wallet, and judging by the pencilled date on the back the most recent one. 'It looks as though our Mr Bradwell had a big notion of himself.'

'Some people can't stay out of photographic studios. It's the curse of the age.' Jarrett took the card-mounted picture and studied it closely. There was no doubt whatsoever that the man leaning on a low Corinthian column in front of a painted scene was Elisha Bradwell, but unusually for posed photographs, he was looking rather pleased with himself. 'J. J. McHugh, Photographic Artist, 29 Jamaica Street.'

'Sadly, it isn't enough for a positive identification, Superintendent,' Inspector Grant suggested. 'Neither of you saw him in life and I was elsewhere.'

'True.' Jarrett returned the portrait to Tommy Quinn. 'Find the girl, Sergeant, but don't let anyone see her identifying Bradwell.'

'Right away, sir.'

'That,' Inspector Grant said as Quinn headed off down the long, thickly carpeted hallway to the stairs and the foyer below, 'is more luck in one minute than I have had since Gilbert Hayes managed to get himself shot.'

Jarrett nodded his agreement.

'You are going to have to let Bain go, Inspector,' he said. 'Everything points to his being falsely incriminated and there is no evidence of his being guilty of any misdemeanour. If we take what you've got to the Fiscal he'll throw it out.'

'Yes, and me with it,' Grant said sadly. 'Truth is, I never for a moment thought the man was guilty. He was just all we had.'

'Perhaps Williamson and Russell will come up with something. Whoever killed Hayes must have made a mistake, however small. No crime is perfect.'

'And no detective, either.'

It took Tommy Quinn a good ten minutes to locate Moira Pearce, secure her affirmation that the photograph was of Elisha Bradwell, then get back to room 205.

'No doubt whatsoever, Superintendent,' he said, clearly pleased with himself. 'This is our latest victim.'

'And the last, hopefully.'

Bit by bit they searched every drawer, document wallet and piece of hand luggage, and did so thoroughly because even a small scrap of information could point to the murderer of these two men. In truth although he had no justification for believing in Gideon Mallam's guilt, Henry Jarrett wanted to find some link to the Guatemalan consul.

What Charlie Grant did find, however, did not raise their spirits. It was a pistol case for a .44 LeMat revolver.

'It borders on the uncanny,' Henry Jarrett said grimly. 'Both men were armed when they went out to meet their destiny, yet they were somehow subdued, stripped naked and gutted. At no time did they attempt to retaliate.'

'A single short blow with a neddy above and behind the right ear, sir,' Tommy Quinn offered, perhaps needlessly, since nothing else made sense. 'That would render anybody unconscious for as long as it takes.'

'Nobody is disputing that,' Jarrett said, his tone revealing the impatience he felt. 'What makes less sense is why two armed men, clearly experienced in the treacherous ways of the world, would lower their guard and permit the assailant to get behind them. They must have suspected that they were going to meet someone who was less than trustworthy and very possibly a threat, or they would not have taken their guns with them.'

'Surely numerous occasions would have presented themselves, sir,' Quinn said in an attempt at salvaging at least a little credibility. 'Or a second attacker waiting in the shadows perhaps.'

Charlie Grant, who had been on the verge of suggesting just that, was relieved when the young sergeant's proposal did not meet Jarrett's approval.

'In Kirchner's case Dr Hamilton's findings point to only one person dragging the body down the slope to the boathouse.' Jarrett glared at him angrily, then continued, 'As far as Bradwell is concerned, Rufus Fogarty swears that two men went upstairs, but only one came back down.'

Tommy Quinn gave a long sigh.

'My apologies, Superintendent,' he said. 'But I think we have to conclude that they were distracted just long enough for the murderer to strike.'

'Distracted? A woman, you mean?'

'It would certainly make sense, sir,' Charlie Grant put in, judging that it was safe now to do so. 'She could have been present on both occasions when they were struck down, but probably not during the disembowelling ceremony.'

'A woman of the night, obviously,' the superintendent said. 'A few extra shillings to decoy a pigeon wouldn't go amiss. A lot of these girls work in league with cosh boys.'

'But not as far as murder, sir.'

'She wouldn't know about that, would she? But the irony is that this unknown female, if indeed she does exist, will be the one who carries the can. The murderer — whether it be Mallam or someone else — is presenting himself as being insane. But this woman could expect no mercy from a jury once they knew what she was and how she lured men to their deaths. Mark my words, she'll hang.'

'That, sir,' Inspector Grant stated firmly, 'is not going to make finding her very easy. With that lying ahead of her I don't think she'd hold her hand up and be counted.'

'Which is why she mustn't know about the

murders, Inspector.'

Tommy Quinn had been mulling this over.

'How are we to prove this theory, sir?' he asked, trying to keep the sarcasm out of his voice. 'There are thousands of streetwalkers, every one of whom distrusts the law absolutely. We, on the other, are few and far between.'

'Sergeant Quinn,' Jarrett pointed out, 'it was your suggestion that both men were distracted. Now it is up to you to find out exactly how.'

'Yes, but — ?

'Just find her, Sergeant Quinn, and do it soon, because if it is not Mallam we have nothing else to go on, and for all we know the lunatic might already be sharpening his sacrificial blade.'

'I thought you wanted me to watch Mallam, sir.'

'You have already found out about the regime he represents and that was good work. Now, Inspector Grant and I will work out the best way to keep an eye on him. But we can't afford to be too sure about anything. If the decoy does exist we have to find her now.'

9

There was a gentle rap at Jarrett's office door and Acting DC Chapman responded instantly to a call to enter.

'Forgive me, Superintendent,' he said, glancing nervously at Charlie Grant, who was not overly delighted at the interruption, 'but I may have hit on an important connection.'

'Really?' Jarrett, who had been reclining, but now sat forward abruptly and waved the lad forward. 'Let's have it, young fellow.'

'Well, sir, there is a name that has cropped up in the papers of both Johannes Kirchner and Elisha Bradwell, and that is Peter Rice. Kirchner had scribbled it on a loose sheet and underlined it three times. Bradwell printed it at the back of a notebook and wrote 'Is this a starter?' beside it. I'm afraid that's all, sir.'

'I would say you have excelled yourself, lad. You seem to have an eye for making connections. Now, carry on with your examination of the ephemera and let me know if you find any other links.' When the young man had departed Jarrett turned to Charlie Grant. 'Peter Rice?'

'It may be a coincidence, Superintendent, but that's the name of Jake McGovern's top reporter. Something of a terrier. When he gets his teeth into something he doesn't let up.'

Jarrett gave this some thought.

'Very well, Inspector,' he said at length, 'I want you to take a couple of uniformed officers and get over to the *Advertiser* office. If this Peter Rice character isn't there find out where he is and bring him in.'

'Under caution?'

'No, too soon. Make him out to be a material witness, but neither he nor McGovern must hear about what happened to Kirchner and Bradwell. Above all else, they must be kept in the dark about that.'

★　★　★

Tommy Quinn had spoken to more tarts than a sailor looking for a bargain, and had long since come to the conclusion that Superintendent Henry Jarrett, good fellow that he was, could be insufferably pig-headed when he wanted to be. He, Sergeant Quinn, had not intended his remark about the killer's victims being distracted by a streetwalker to be taken literally word for word. What he intended was that in his estimation hardened adventurers like Kirchner and Bradwell

217

would not have been easily ambushed, particularly as both were armed and obviously anticipating trouble.

He had more or less agreed with himself that he would give up when he reached Montrose Street and retire to the nearest coffee house, where he would rest his feet and wait until his shift came to an end. If he grumbled pathetically and looked sufficiently forlorn when he returned to the office, perhaps Jarrett would see sense and abandon what was clearly a futile and time-wasting search.

The young woman had treated herself to a moth-eaten feather boa in a vain attempt at looking respectable. But the red cheeks and lips, plus the fact that she was obviously not going anywhere, spoke volumes.

When Tommy Quinn approached she smiled broadly, but her expression turned sour when he produced the badge.

'Since when did they start using detectives on the beat?' she asked.

'This isn't a round-up,' Quinn said. 'I'm seeking information about an attack on a gentleman.'

'What sort of attack?'

'Cosh. Probably bundled into a vehicle and spirited away.'

She eyed him cautiously for a time, as if

trying to figure out how much she should say
without getting herself embroiled.

'Is there anything in it?'

'A few bob for the right information.
Perhaps a sovereign.'

'In that case I might just have seen
something, but it had nothing to do with me,
you understand.'

'So you weren't a decoy?'

The girl's eyes widened.

'Perish the thought,' she breathed. 'I know
what would happen to me if the law thought
I'd been part of it. Accessory, that's what
they'd make me out to be. And if the victim
was a gent like you say it would go all the
worse for me.'

'Just tell me what you know,' Tommy
Quinn said. 'I won't even ask your name, so
you have nothing to fear.'

'Is that a promise?'

'Absolutely. Help me solve this one and
you can scurry off.'

'With my money?'

'Of course.'

'Here and now? I'm not going to any cop
shop for it.'

'You are supposed to collect it from the
desk,' Sergeant Quinn replied. 'Strictly
speaking, I am not allowed to hand money
over to someone in your line of work. You

should know that by now.'

The girl shrugged.

'No money, no story.'

'Very well. The law doesn't say anything about me losing money and you finding it. Now, tell me what you know.'

'Well, it was just over there by the arches,' she said. 'Late evening, it was. I was here as usual, when a pony and cart arrived and pulled up across the road. It was a businessman's private buggy. A town dog-cart. I see a lot of them. They're not big like your four-wheeled landed sort drive. More your merchant type with a single pony. Anyway, they probably didn't see me, because I always keep myself in the shadows and away from the bluebottles until a client comes along, and then I make my presence known, if you see what I mean.'

'How many were in the buggy?'

'Two. I thought at first it was a bit of sport they were after, but they made no attempt to come across. Instead, one of them pointed to a dark arch, and when the other turned in that direction he whacked him. The man dropped like a stone.'

'No headwear?'

'The one dishing out the cosh had a topper, but the poor bugger who took the thump was bare-headed.'

'What happened then?'

'The attacker bundled the unconscious character into the back of the dog cart, threw a tarp or sheet over him and was on his merry way. But don't ask me what it was all about, because I couldn't make head nor tail of it.'

'I don't suppose you reported the incident?' Tommy Quinn ventured.

The girl gave a short, sardonic laugh.

'What did I tell you about me and cop shops?' she said. 'Of course I didn't report it. Told a few of the other girls, though. You always spread good stories about.'

'Did any of them have similar experiences?'

'Well, there are plenty of cosh boys around, looking for stray gents who are out of their depth, but when one gent lays another low that's a different thing altogether. I don't think any of the girls had ever heard of that.'

'And was that the only time you witnessed such a thing?'

'How many times has it happened? I mean, is this some kind of lunatic?'

'Twice,' Tommy admitted. 'We know of two occasions.'

'I only saw it the once. Of course, I'm not here all the time.'

'Very well, a description, if you will. What can you remember about the two men?'

'Well, the one with the cosh was sort of

tallish and quite thin, but toppers make men bigger, don't they. That's what they're for, I'm told.'

Impatient with the girl's tendency to drift from the point, Sergeant Quinn said, 'Forget about that. What did he look like? Did he have facial hair?'

'I couldn't see clearly from over here. I think he was clean-shaven, but it's hard to say.'

'And the other one?'

'He was slightly shorter and he didn't have either a beard or moustache, only sideburns. I think his hair was very light, but the gas lamp sometimes does that, doesn't it?'

Tommy nodded.

'Just one last thing,' he said. 'What direction did the vehicle take?'

'Oh, that's easy. Westward. He swung in a tight circle and made off right past me, but I was still in the shadows and I wasn't going to make my presence known. An individual like that isn't going to leave a witness if he can help it.'

'Please, just tell me where he went.'

'He swung into Cochrane Street, so he must have been heading out to the West End, unless he was making for one of the big houses near George Square.'

Tommy dug into his waistcoat fob pocket

and produced the sovereign which he had managed to talk Superintendent Jarrett into allocating for good information. This he balanced on his thumbnail and flipped into the air, but almost immediately her right hand snaked out and claimed it.

It wasn't the same as placing it on her open palm, and that was all the law demanded of him.

* ★ ★

Even terror has its limits. Sooner or later the cowed creature will turn on its oppressor in a last ditch attempt at breaking free of the cage of fear. It will do this when deep down it comes to believe that it would be better dead than living with torment.

Peter Rice reached that point quite quickly. It was made easier by the realization that his self-imposed incarceration in the small room almost certainly meant the loss of the fortune he had dreamt of for so long. It was just possible that the whole dreadful scene he had witnessed had been staged to scare off the likes of him, but deep down he knew that this wasn't so. It was real all right and his own importance in the scheme of things was not as great as he'd imagined. Like it or not, Peter Rice was small beer in the hunt for the Jade King.

Cautiously, and still fighting fear, he set a fire in the register grate, filled his iron kettle from the water pail and pressed it into the coals. When it boiled he poured the scalding water into the chipped enamel basin and set about stropping his Mappin and Webb cutthroat razor. It was time to pull himself together and put in an appearance at the office, although exactly how much he was willing to tell Editor McGovern was not something he had yet decided.

After he had washed, shaved and donned his only other suit, he made a loose parcel out of the one that had suffered much wear and tear in his speedy departure from the scene of horror, and left the small dwelling, but carefully, having first made sure that there were no monsters waiting for him outside the door.

His intention was to first deposit the garments with the cleaner to have the small rip mended and the grass stains removed, then report to Jake McGovern with the story he had thought up while scratching his chin. Such absences from the office were not unusual at his level, but Editor McGovern's tolerance was not unlimited. He would expect to hear something, however limited, and would need assurance that a good story was in the offing.

Rice drew the door closed, secured the simple lock and dropped the key into his pocket. Considering how little he had to lose, a double-throw mortise would have been both expensive and unnecessary. As always, he pushed the door a couple of times to make sure it really was tight against a thieving world.

He turned, began to descend the old, creaky treads, but almost immediately found himself frozen to the spot, his fingers tightly clutching the worn handrail. Although he could not see fully into the grey shadows of the half-landing he could make out what he took to be the shapes of three men, just waiting to pounce as soon as he was close enough to be seized. Instinctively then, he turned and began to clamber back up the stairs, his right hand now buried deep in his pocket in search of the key, his throat uttering almost animalistic squeals of terror.

But there was to be no escape. Behind him there was a flurry of boots on the worn timber and a powerful grip took hold of his coat, dragging him backwards and causing him to completely lose his footing.

'Just calm down, Mr Rice,' Charlie Grant said evenly. 'Surrender your key to the constables so that they can search your abode, while you and I take the wagon back to headquarters. Promise me you won't try to flee and I won't put the restraints on you.'

★ ★ ★

A thoroughly miserable Albert Sweetman listened to the footsteps as they approached his tiny room, and not for the first time in his life felt that calamity was imminent. Indeed, a nagging anticipation of disaster was his constant companion in life, and the only thing he could honestly rely upon.

This time he had no need to imagine impending doom. Just a few minutes earlier he had peered through his tiny window and watched them arrive: a large, well-built young fellow and a much shorter, bow-legged man of the cloth, carrying a Bible large enough to sit on. Now fate had made its way up the stairs and was at his very door. This time there would be no more excuses, no more buying time.

Then the door flew open and Eileen McCreedy scurried in, her right hand reaching for his wrinkled shirt front and her left for the coat he had been using as an extra blanket.

'Move yourself!' she ordered, while trying to keep her voice low. 'Hurry up in the name of God!'

'But — '

'No buts, you've got to get out of here.' Her eyes flashed as she bundled him backwards out into the narrow hallway. 'Big Dugald MacLeish is home from the sea and he's brought the minister with him. She's just about fit to be tied because she doesn't think Dugald's good enough for me, but he's determined and so am I. Now you've got to get out of here or it'll be the worse for you.'

'You mean I'm free?' Sweetman blurted.

'Oh, be quiet and get out. Big Dugald can be very jealous and if he gets it into his head that you've been taking liberties he'll break your neck, fat as it is.'

Still not quite sure that he was awake, Albert paused at the top of the stairs until Eileen forced him to descend to the foyer by pushing him again and again.

'Where are they?' he asked over his shoulder.

'In the good room. That's where we're going to have the ceremony and there's nothing she can do about it. She won't tell them about you because there would be too much explaining to do, so get down with you and be gone.'

Before he quite realized it, he was outside in the cool air, alone and clutching a bundle to his chest that consisted of his coat, waistcoat and carpet bag. Behind him the front door crashed shut and a large slip bolt announced that no one would be admitted in the foreseeable future.

It seemed as though months had passed since he'd arrived at this place, but he gathered his wits and soon made off down the winding path to the rutted byway that served as a road between Port Rannald and Invercoll. At this point there was really no need to choose direction. He was in no fit state to continue his calls, so, no matter what Mr Hall might say, Albert Sweetman started to trot in the direction of Port Rannald, from where he would return to Glasgow and the safety of Mrs Maitland's superior guest-house for single gentlemen.

★ ★ ★

Superintendent Henry Jarrett and Sergeant Quinn were discussing the street girl's account when Inspector Grant escorted Peter Rice along the corridor in the direction of the interrogation room. Even though the windows above dado level allowed Jarrett to see all the comings and goings, Charlie Grant nevertheless rapped on the door and announced that he had brought Rice in, so whenever the superintendent was ready they would be in the interview room.

Jarrett acknowledged this with a wave and Charlie Grant continued on his way.

'What do you think, Sergeant Quinn?' he asked.

Quinn shook his head. It was not a good beginning.

'The girl described the attacker as tallish and thin. That doesn't fit the inspector's prisoner at all.'

'No, but it does fit Gideon Mallam, so I want you to return to keeping him under surveillance, but now you must also find out what kind of buggy he drives, if any. I'm not sure how you are going to check his movements on the evenings of the two murders, but discretion is the order of the day. He mustn't know you've got your eye on him.' Jarrett rose from his chair and crossed to the door. 'If the girl's description can be relied upon, Peter Rice is not a murder suspect, but I still want to know why his name cropped up in the writings of both victims.'

'That isn't the only thing that bothers me, sir,' Tommy Quinn offered. 'Why would the killer lay Johannes Kirchner low in one place, drive him to another destination to perform his insane ceremony, then move the body to the boathouse? Dr Hamilton has stated that

Kirchner couldn't possibly have been killed where he was found because of the almost total absence of blood. Bradwell, on the other hand, was killed in Fogarty's hotel and just left there.'

'If you are suggesting that there are two separate lunatics, Sergeant,' Jarrett said firmly, 'I cannot accept it.'

'No. Not two killers, Superintendent, just a change in *modus operandi*. It's as though he is getting more confident.'

'You are not a mind-doctor, Sergeant Quinn, and neither am I. We are concerned only with provable facts. Where was Mallam when the men were murdered? Did he have motive and opportunity? We leave his state of mind to the doctors and the law courts. It has nothing to do with us.'

* * *

As expected, Peter Rice was looking thoroughly dejected when Henry Jarrett entered the interrogation room and took his seat beside Charlie Grant.

'This is Superintendent Jarrett,' Grant said. 'He is the senior officer and will be conducting this interview.'

Rice nodded.

'I know who you are, Superintendent,' he

230

said. 'It's my job to know.'

'And what exactly is your job, Mr Rice?'

'Please, I'm not a fool. You know what I do and who I work for, but how did you know where I live?'

'Jake McGovern,' Charlie Grant replied casually. 'You've been with the *Advertiser* for long enough to know that, if threatened, McGovern will throw someone else to the lions.'

'He told you where to find me?'

'Of course. As soon as he found out that you were under investigation by the police he didn't want any part of it.'

'Well, that's very kind of you. It appears that you have just destroyed my career.' Peter Rice drove his fingers through his thick brown hair. 'What investigation? I haven't done anything wrong.'

'That remains to be seen,' Jarrett stated. 'Anyway, we will ask the questions, if you don't mind. First, why did our officers find notes relating to Johannes Kirchner and Elisha Bradwell in your room? Conversely, why would your name be on papers belonging to these two individuals?'

Rice spread his arms to indicate confusion.

'It's quite beyond me, Superintendent,' he said, his tone indicating a desire to please. 'I'm sorry, but I can't help you.'

'Nonsense. You wrote their names down. You also noted their addresses, so how can you possibly say that you can't help us?'

'Perhaps I should have said that it probably wasn't all that important. I make a note of a lot of names and facts, most of which turn out to be irrelevant. And as far as my name being known to these other individuals, why don't you ask them?'

Jarrett resisted the temptation to glance at Charlie Grant, but he could tell that the inspector had been equally struck by Rice's sincerity. Unless he was the best actor since Edmund Keane, the newspaperman did not know that Kirchner and Bradwell were dead.

But Rice's ignorance did not end there. When Jarrett placed a folded copy of the *Advertiser* on the table before him and pointed to the police request for Bradwell to put in an appearance, the journalist simply peered at it for a few moments, then looked the superintendent straight in the eye.

'I don't understand,' he said quietly. 'What is this all about?'

'Are you telling us that you did not see this item? It's the paper you work for, Rice. How stupid do you think I am?'

'No, you don't understand. I've been unwell for the last few days. I sent a note to Mr McGovern to that effect, although it wasn't really necessary. It's quite common for a lead reporter to follow a story through, so he wouldn't have queried my absence.'

'Where were you off to when Inspector Grant and his men encountered you on the stairs?'

'Encountered?' Rice gave a snort. 'That's putting it nicely. I nearly shit myself.'

'Why?'

'Because they scared me half to death, that's why.'

'I'm sorry, Mr Rice, but you overreacted and I want to know why. Who did you think they were?'

'I don't know. Robbers, I suppose.'

'Would you honestly describe your building as being an attraction to thieves? I hardly think so.' Jarrett swept the *Advertiser* aside and slapped a palm on the wooden surface. 'Come on, now. Who or what did you think was waiting for you? Not the police, I'm sure, because you don't have a criminal record. So who could scare you that much?'

'I . . . don't know.'

'Of course you know. I don't believe for a minute that you were unwell. I think you were lying low and eventually decided that it was safe to venture forth.'

'That isn't true.' Peter Rice was sweating profusely now. Jarrett's guesses were so accurate that it was almost as though he was looking into the man's mind. 'I hadn't been well and was still in a nervous state.'

'So it was a nervous condition, Mr Rice, and not a physical one? Overwork, perhaps?'

'I have been working long hours, Superintendent.'

'Doing what? Trying to steal a march on Kirchner and Bradwell, perhaps?'

'I don't know what you mean.'

'Of course you do. Indeed, I would venture to suggest that you already had your sights set on a particular prize even before these two arrived and threatened your plans.'

'That just isn't true.'

'Isn't it?' Charlie Grant put in loudly. 'Kirchner and Bradwell had only one thing on their minds, so if they troubled even to write your name it means that you are on the same track.'

Peter Rice stared at him, then at Jarrett.

'Had?' he breathed. 'Christ Almighty, they're dead, aren't they?'

'Just a slip of the tongue,' the inspector said, but he knew it was too late.

'No, it was no slip of the tongue. I'm here because they're dead and you're desperate for someone to pin it on.'

Since there was no point in continuing to deny it, Jarrett said, 'Allow me to rephrase that, Mr Rice. You are here because you and you alone can be linked to Kirchner and Bradwell.'

'There is one other.'

'And that is?'

'Whoever killed them.'

Jarrett smiled thinly.

'I didn't say they were killed.'

'It stands to reason, doesn't it? Two perfectly healthy individuals aren't suddenly going to pop their clogs.' Rice paused, then continued, 'How did they die, anyway?'

'Don't you know?'

'No, of course I don't know. I could take a guess at it and say they were shot. Am I right?'

Jarrett didn't confirm this, but instead asked, 'Are you willing to say where you were on each of the last five evenings?'

'Why five?'

'Please answer me, Mr Rice. Tell us what you were doing on each of those evenings and whether anyone can confirm it.'

'Well, the short answer is just what I have already told you. I was laid up with the shivers and belly pains. As far as anyone being able to substantiate this is concerned, no, there's no one. I rarely see the other inhabitants of the building, and the landlord only puts in an appearance if the rent is in arrears.'

'That puts you in a very difficult position.' Charlie Grant lifted the loose parcel from the floor by his boot and laid it in the middle of the table. 'How did this suit get into the mess it is? You're not a labouring man by any means, so what have you been playing at?'

'Inspector,' Rice began in a slow, purposeful tone, 'like you, I am an investigator. That often means endless trudging and sometimes climbing walls, crawling through bushes until you tear the backside out of your trousers and generally getting up to much of what any small boy would be proud of.'

'Such as burgling Dr Hamilton's laboratory at the mortuary?' Henry Jarrett asked unexpectedly.

Rice was visibly taken aback.

'Certainly not, Superintendent,' he said firmly. 'That would be strictly against the law.'

'Agreed, but allow me to ask you again. Did you break into the mortuary?'

'No, I did not. Anyone might have rifled his files. Why single me out?'

'Who said anything about rifling the files?'

For a few moments Peter Rice was at a loss for words.

'It stands to reason,' he finally managed. 'What else would a burglar want? There isn't a great demand for corpses any more.'

'Mr Rice,' Jarrett was now reaching the end of his patience, 'I don't think you realize how much trouble you are in. Not only has your name been linked to Kirchner and Bradwell, but your activities, and explanations, are highly suspect. I don't believe for a moment that you were ill, so if you wish to remove all suspicion of your involvement in murder you must tell me exactly what you have been up to and why we found your name in the personal papers of the deceased.'

It took quite some time and a great deal of hand-wringing before Peter Rice had gathered together his thoughts and was ready to present what he hoped would be an acceptable story.

'Very well,' he said, trusting his narrative would sound plausible to these individuals who had heard every lie in the book. 'Some time ago, I stumbled across what appeared at first to be the sort of myth that can be retold anywhere. Working for Jake McGovern means that I'm always on the look-out for the more sensational sort of stuff. You know the kind of thing: monsters that live in the sewers and thrive on rats, grey giants that loom out of the fog and the legendary Pictish tunnels beneath the city. All nonsense, of course.

'Then McGovern heard about the treasure

story and got very excited about the whole idea. From that moment on I was assigned solely to that one investigation. He wanted some tangible proof, however flimsy, that he could pad out and use in a series of articles. The more days he could ring out of it the better.

'That was when I discovered that professional treasure-seekers had moved in and were taking the matter seriously. The reason for their interest was an article written by the pathologist, Dr Hamilton, in which he seemed to confirm something they had already been working on. Naturally, I located these adventurers and interviewed them for the *Advertiser*, and that is why their names are in my notebook, and I dare say why they troubled to make a note of mine.'

Jarrett leaned back, folded his arms and considered Peter Rice for a half-minute or so.

'Good,' he said at length, 'but perhaps a shade too perfect. Most people don't have all the answers, Mr Rice, just as innocent people cannot always account for their whereabouts at any given moment of any day.'

'And neither could I, Superintendent,' Rice said. 'If you were to ask me where I ate lunch the Wednesday before last I doubt if I could remember. But these interviews stuck in my mind because neither man was willing to talk and clearly regarded me as a fly in the ointment.'

'Do you still deny breaking into the mortuary?'

'As God's my witness.' Rice adopted his hurt face. 'Why on earth should it have to be me? Surely Kirchner or Bradwell are more likely candidates? They were the treasure-seekers, not I, so they would require the information.'

'What information, Mr Rice?'

For a moment or two Peter Rice was again at a loss for words, but soon recovered his composure.

'Whatever information they deemed sufficiently important to risk breaking the law to get.'

'And you have no idea what that could be?'

'None whatsoever.'

Although Jarrett was sure that Peter Rice was not telling him everything, and that what little he had offered might itself be questionable, he couldn't see the man as the killer. To begin with, if the street-girl was any judge he was too short. Next, it was the collective opinion of the detectives that the man who committed the crimes was not normal, yet Rice exhibited none of the signs Jarrett might have expected to see. He had spoken to numerous irrational killers in his time and at some stage in the conversation there had been a sudden, unexpected outburst of the sort that characterises paranoiacs and religious fanatics. But there was no indication at all of Rice being a troubled soul. On top of that, the officers who searched his billet failed to find even the smallest indicator of serious wrongdoing.

Most important of all, though, as far as Henry Jarrett was concerned was his own feeling. From the moment he entered the interrogation room and took his place across the table from Rice he had known instinctively that this was not the man.

'What are we going to do with you, Mr Rice?' the superintendent asked quietly.

'Let me go, of course.' Peter Rice smiled and nodded at the senior officers in turn. 'I can see how you might have thought it strange that I should have been known to two murdered men, but I think I have explained that quite satisfactorily.'

'Yes, but that is hardly the point, is it? We are in an awkward position. The untimely deaths of Kirchner and Bradwell are known only to a small number of officers, and that was how we planned to keep it so that the murderer would be denied that which we believe is most important to him — publicity. This man, whoever he is, must be raging at not terrifying the city in the way he probably wants to. But that is only because we have so far kept the details from Jake McGovern. If I let you go it will only be a matter of hours before the *Advertiser* is on the pavement with the biggest story it has had since the cholera outbreak.'

Rice nodded.

'You are afraid that I am going to run straight to McGovern,' he said.

'Aren't you? He is your lord and master, after all, the one who provides your daily crust. When you were brought in you didn't have much to offer him, but that has changed now. Two treasure seekers are dead and McGovern is the very man to link the murders to the jade mask and his own sensational story about curses and God knows what. Never one to miss the opportunity to keep the pot boiling, your editor.'

'What if I gave you my word that I would keep it to myself?'

'I dare say you would be more than happy to give such an assurance, Mr Rice, but why should you keep it? Just give me one good reason why a newspaperman should fail to capitalize on what is probably the best story that has come his way in a long time.'

'Very well,' Rice said sincerely, 'let's say

that I would be happy to keep this under wraps in exchange for the whole story when you get this man. I could give Jake McGovern the few sketchy facts I know, and leave him to concoct some fanciful nonsense, or I could hold my peace and present him with the entire case, *fait accompli*, and tied up with a big ribbon.'

Jarrett and Grant exchanged glances, then the inspector said, 'We need more than a verbal guarantee.'

'I can't imagine what that might be.'

'A written confession regarding the break-in at the mortuary.'

'But I've already told you . . .'

'I know what you've told us, Mr Rice,' Jarrett put in, 'and I also know what we assume happened.'

'That is?'

'According to our information, Dr Hamilton did not reveal the exact spot where the servant was buried. That was the one missing detail in what became known as the Hamilton Question. Correct me if I'm wrong, Mr Rice, but either Kirchner or Bradwell had something you wanted and the price for getting it was the whereabouts of the old gravesite.'

Peter Rice looked down as his clasped hands and mulled this over, while the detectives watched and gave him enough time to collect his thoughts.

'If I signed a confession,' he said, 'I could get five years in Duke Street Prison.'

'Only if we used such a confession. As things stand, the murders are considerably more important than your little bout of burglary.'

'At the moment, yes, but you would have a sword over my head ever after. The first time I got under your feet you would dig that out and use it against me.'

'Not quite, Mr Rice. The Fiscal would want to know why it had not been used sooner, so it will be useful only for a few days and then it will be consigned to the fire.'

Rice considered this, then nodded his agreement.

'I have no choice, Superintendent,' he said. 'What do you want me to write?'

'Just what led up to the break-in, what exactly the arrangement was and anything you might know about the deaths of Kirchner and Bradwell.'

'I don't know anything about that.'

'Then put down everything you do know about those two, leaving nothing out. And remember, if you lie we'll be on to it right away.'

It was all Charlie Grant could do to keep from bursting out laughing, but somehow he kept a straight, even dour, expression and sat silently as Peter Rice covered the best part of one side of a foolscap sheet with his small, precise handwriting.

When it was finished and signed and the pen was returned to the writing set in the middle of the table, Rice spun his part-truth, part-fable around and pushed it across to Jarrett.

'That's it, Superintendent,' he said resignedly. 'There is nothing else. It's all there.'

Jarrett studied the paper for some time, then passed it to Charlie Grant.

'Very well, Mr Rice,' he said, 'you're free to go, but unless you have a desperate need to call in at the *Advertiser* offices, give McGovern a wide berth until we say otherwise.'

10

It was not the first time that the solution to a crime had come to Inspector Charlie Grant right out of the proverbial blue. In fact, he had noticed on several occasions that the harder he worried at a case the less likely it was that he would benefit from inspiration. It was only when he put his feet up, told himself that he was going to hand the whole thing over to someone else and just enjoy a well-deserved spot of relaxation that the answer seemed to come out of nowhere. And so it was with the Gilbert Hayes killing at the fairground. In truth, the solution was both obvious and timely. Superintendent Jarrett wanted him to get this matter wrapped up and out of the way so that he could concentrate on a potentially much more serious problem. Put another way, Jarrett did not feel that the Chief Constable would be quite as concerned about the Hayes killing as he would be over a madman with a penchant for human hearts. So far they had managed to contain the whole thing, but that wouldn't be possible for much longer, and certainly not forever.

They arrived at the tent within minutes of each other, partly because they had been asked to gather there by DCs Williamson and Russell on Charlie Grant's orders, but mainly because they couldn't afford not to be there.

Inspector Grant let his eyes travel over the assembled troupe — William Blundell, Sam Hicks, Clarence Moultrie, Emma Saunter, Rupert Vidler and Thomas Weaver — but each face still wore the same impenetrable expression he encountered whenever he interviewed them. No one was going to break down and admit to anything. That much he knew. Just as he was certain that they would not confirm the theory he was about to put to them.

'I am not getting any younger,' he told them, 'and one of these days they are going to ask for my badge. What am I going to do then, I ask myself. Recently I thought of an answer. I could put all my experience of chasing villains to good use by writing Penny Dreadfuls. I even have my first one thought out.

'It's about a murder at a fairground. A money-lender is shot to death, but why and by whom? The problem is, you see, that there is no real motive, which is something every good murder must have. It is all very well saying that one of his clients was fed up

246

paying him two hard-earned pounds a week and decided to end it quickly and cleanly. But why risk the gallows for such a paltry sum when it was only a matter of time before the debt was paid off. People tend not to kill money-lenders.

'But what if there was no prospect of it ever being paid off? What if, on the contrary, the payments were about to go up, and up, and up?' Charlie paused briefly and waited in vain for some sign that he had hit a raw nerve. 'What if the dead man was not a money-lender at all, but a blackmailer?'

Charlie produced Gilbert Hayes's account-book, let it fall open to reveal the little silver key he had been using as a marker, then placed both items on Sam Hicks' photographic desk, the key perfectly positioned in the middle of the black book.

'Of course, it isn't just one of the blackmailer's victims who desires his death more than anything,' he went on, 'it is all of them. Normally, they would not be acquainted with each other, but in a close-knit environment like a fairground everyone has a good idea of what is going on. So they meet to discuss their desperate plight and arrive at an excellent solution. They will kill the monster in such a way that no one but the shooter knows who actually pulled the trigger. That way no one can give the proverbial game away.

'What they do is this: they hold a draw, with each person selecting one of six paper folds. One has to obtain a gun and the accoutrements, another must lead the blackmailer to the scene of his demise, yet another will meantime gain entry to the man's caravan, where it is believed that the evidence against each of them must be hidden, a fourth must retrieve the firearm from the murder site and dispose of it. The fifth and sixth folds are blank as befits all proper draws.

'The entire thing goes off swimmingly, except for two minor hitches. Before the one who was due to get rid of the gun — no doubt in the river — the party realize that a fellow stallholder is being too cosy with my hero, the investigating police officer. The other snag is that the proof of their misdeeds cannot be found in the blackmailer's van. They have certainly killed him, but they have not managed to destroy the evidence or lay hands on his book, which contains their initials and a record of their payments.

'In desperation, they attempt to incriminate the one they wrongly believe to be a police informer. This merely makes my hero very, very suspicious. He realizes that panic has set in and people who panic make mistakes.

248

'But he also realizes something much more to the point. The silver key belongs to a safe deposit box in which the damning proof is almost certainly hidden. That box could be in any bank in any town from Land's End to John O' Groats, and there are thousands of them. Without that box there would be no possibility of obtaining a conviction, because a ledger of initials proves nothing at all.'

Inspector Grant slowly strolled to the flap-door of the tent, where DCs Williamson and Russell were waiting, but before departing he turned again to the still impassive faces and said, 'I'll leave those items with you. It is entirely up to you to decide what you want to do with them, but I know what I would do.'

He paused outside the tent and carefully stepped over and around some of the more daunting muddy puddles.

'Back to headquarters?' he asked over his shoulder. 'Or are you happy where you are?'

'I thought I might pack it in and become a juggler, sir,' Williamson replied, grinning.

'Don't try to be a joker, sonny. It doesn't bloody well suit you.'

★   ★   ★

Detective Sergeant Tommy Quinn took a chair at Superintendent Jarrett's bidding and promptly produced his notebook.

'Gideon Norman Mallam,' he said, while his boss leaned back and listened carefully. 'Forty-four years of age, unmarried, former importer of timber from Central America, sold his business to Baird & Brown of Port Dundas, and is now in a state of semi-retirement. As a result of his numerous contacts in Guatemala he was offered the position of consul to that country.'

'Residence?'

'Hillview, Clairemont Drive. He keeps a small staff.' Tommy smiled broadly. 'According to his milk delivery man, the cook does not think very highly of him. A mean so-and-so, in fact.'

'Did you find out anything about his social life?'

'Member of the Bath Street Literary Society and the Gentleman's Photographic Club.' Sergeant Quinn flipped over a sheet. 'Doesn't keep a driver. Uses Hansoms for travelling back and forth to the office, and for his evenings out.'

'That doesn't prove anything. It is extremely easy to hire a buggy, Sergeant.' Henry Jarrett was quite determined to keep Mallam firmly in his sights. 'Anything else on the man?'

'Not a great deal, sir.' Tommy Quinn was pensive for a few moments. 'To be honest,

Superintendent, I don't think Mallam is our man.'

'Really? Why not?'

'Well, for one thing the killer must have been blood-drenched. Dr Hamilton as much as said that. Now, to the best of our knowledge no one saw the Kirchner murder, but Rufus Fogarty had a good look at the man who murdered Elisha Bradwell and there was no sign of blood on him.'

'Because Bradwell was dead, and corpses don't gush when the pump has ceased. If you recall, Bradwell's skull was thin, a physical anomaly that has sent quite a few cosh boys to the gallows.'

'His hands would still have been bloody underneath his gloves. What I am trying to say, Superintendent, is that someone in Mallam's household would have spotted traces of blood, whether it was on his clothes or the wash-basin.'

'How do you know they didn't?' Jarrett spread his arms and invited a reply. But it was obvious that Sergeant Quinn was momentarily taken aback. 'You are not going to suggest that the servants would immediately run for a beat policeman? No, they would accept his explanation and keep their mouths shut.'

'But Kirchner wasn't dead when he was cut

open. The killer would be in a terrible mess.'

'So? We don't know the circumstances. In fact, we don't know anything except where the body was eventually laid out. The murderer might have had hours to clean himself up.'

Tommy Quinn shook his head and it was clear that he was still sticking to his belief that Mallam was not involved. But Superintendent Henry Jarrett was the boss and whatever he said went.

'What now, sir?' he asked.

'I want Mallam kept under observation. Put Williamson and Russell onto it. And you might as well give young Chapman a taste of boredom.'

But Sergeant Quinn's brief dalliance with mutiny was not quite over.

'With respect, Superintendent,' he said, 'I'm not altogether sure how they are going to do that. Hillview is a detached villa on Clairemont Drive, a tree-lined cul-de-sac in a quiet suburban area. Whether we use a plain van or officers on the pavement, it is going to be obvious to Mallam and everyone else that the property is being watched.'

'There is no great problem,' Jarrett stated flatly. 'Position the detectives at the entrance to the cul-de-sac in an unmarked vehicle, where they can see the arrival and departure of a Hansom.'

Since Tommy Quinn could neither fault nor commend this plan, he quietly withdrew and set about preparing the finer details of the Mallam surveillance operation.

★　★　★

Peter Rice prided himself on being nobody's fool. He knew that Jarrett had not swallowed his parcel of truths and lies, and had let him go only because he could not prove the charge of breaking and entering. As it was, the signed confession was only good for a short time, after which Superintendent Jarrett could be called to account for not acting upon it.

But the most important question in Rice's mind as he sat on the edge of his narrow bed was whether they were being truthful when they assured him that they weren't going to keep an eye on him. According to them, they only had a limited number of detectives, all of whom would be required to investigate more pressing matters. That, of course, meant the killings of Kirchner and Bradwell. Since he had been excluded from any list of suspects they may have been toying with, it was reasonable to assume that he could take them at their word.

As might be expected, his thoughts jumped

back to the hideous killing he had witnessed in the woods, only now he was able to make a guess at the identity of the victim. It was simply too much of a coincidence for it to have been anyone other than Kirchner or Bradwell, since it was there that they had done most of their recent prowling. His first understandable, though irrational, thought was that one of them had been the victim of the other, but as both had perished that was clearly not the case. Anyway, he had seen both men often enough to say for certain that neither was the painted heathen.

Although the monster was still out there, Rice felt himself buoyed up by the knowledge that Kirchner and Bradwell had probably not found the boxes after all. Probably not, he thought, but not certainly not. The killer may have been out to prevent the treasure-hunters from succeeding in their quest, but on the other hand he could have been acting out his fury at having been beaten in the quest.

On balance, Rice concluded it was the former, which meant that the boxes were still waiting to be found, and that he was still at risk if he persisted in attempting to locate them.

Yet there was little else he could do. He was in possession of information known to no other man, information he'd withheld from

Jarrett and Grant, information that he had gleaned from the letters of his mother's great-grandfather, Lucius Holman, who painstakingly recorded the ravings of the mad Tobias Fisher in the Garngad Asylum. Although Fisher did not reveal the whereabouts of his alleged treasure, sufficient information was contained in Holman's hastily-scrawled sheets to enable an intelligent man to narrow it down to a few properties. And Peter Rice, in his own estimation, was intelligent.

This was more than he was willing to say about the officers who searched his one-roomed dwelling. If Superintendent Jarrett really considered him a suspect in the murders, his place would have received a much more thorough going over, and that would have uncovered sheafs of his own rough calculations. As it was, they found the connection between himself and the treasure seekers, and not much more.

A combination of fact and cold reason told Peter Rice that Fisher's hiding place, if it did indeed exist, was within a quarter of a mile or so of the slain servant's shallow grave. The Hamilton article made it perfectly clear that in the pathologist's estimation the man had been brought down after a pursuit. Peter Rice, on several occasions, had attempted to re-enact just such a chase, and was utterly convinced that the overall distance two untrained men could cover before collapsing was about four hundred yards, and only then if panic or fury were involved.

Within such a radius lay three substantial properties: Greenfield House, Stonewood Mansion and Alder Grange, each of which was hidden from the others by dense forest. These were not the large houses of the landed gentry, with paddocks and rolling fields, but the secluded mansion-houses of city nabobs or colonial merchants.

He rose from the bed and crossed to the window. There was nothing untoward and no sign of police surveillance, so he snatched up his coat and quit the place.

As there was no good reason why he should choose one property over another, he decided to start with Greenfield House.

But that would be a task for the morrow.

★　★　★

Despite the state of war existing between the states of North America and at least two countries in Central America, trade persisted, carriages came and went in Royal Exchange Square, and the Guatemalan Consulate at number 22 received its fair share of callers. But by four in the afternoon Gideon Mallam clearly felt that he had contributed sufficiently to the economy of that far-off land and accordingly locked up his small office and made his way to the Hansom rank at the corner of Queen Street and the Square.

He may very well have been described as a mean so-and-so, but when it came down to himself and his own comfort he was never one for horse-buses, preferring to survey the comings and goings of the lower orders from the quiet seclusion of a trotting cab.

Three doors away from the consulate was the street-level office of British and Irish Magnetic Telegraph Co. From there, DC Russell notified Sergeant Quinn at headquarters that Gideon Mallam had just left. Quinn, for his part, immediately deployed DC Williamson and Acting DC Walter Chapman, along with PC Jamieson atop the wagonette. His job would be to follow Mallam if he left the house.

In the event, it turned out to be a wasted night. Gideon Mallam's bedroom lamp was extinguished at ten and the officers climbed aboard the wagonette and left. Only Domino enjoyed the night out.

11

Peter Rice was too long in the tooth to arrive at Greenfield House without having carried out a certain amount of research. He knew who owned the property, a certain amount about his family and just enough history to make the reason for his visit sound plausible.

The woman who opened the large door as a consequence of his having firmly and confidently pulled the bell chain was tall, sallow-skinned and rather severe.

'The family is not at home,' she told him flatly in response to his request.

'When would it be convenient to see the master of the house?'

She shrugged lightly.

'As soon as he decides to return from St Lucia,' she said. 'That might be about two months from now, but it all depends on the sugar harvest.'

'Then perhaps you can help me.'

'I doubt it, Mr . . . '

'Peter Rice. I'm a journalist.'

If this was intended to placate her it failed miserably.

'What could you possibly want to know

about Mr Thornton?' she demanded. 'And what paper are you from?'

'The *Herald*,' Rice replied. It was a lie he had become accustomed to delivering without hesitation. 'To be perfectly honest, Madam, it isn't Mr Thornton I am interested in. It's the house. My editor has asked me to do a piece on the big houses in the Vale, and I'm sure Mr Thornton would not like it if we omitted to include Greenfield House.'

The change was immediate and dramatic: she no longer blocked his way, but stepped quickly aside and indicated the hallway with a sweep of the hand.

'Mrs Cameron,' she said warmly. 'I am the housekeeper to the Thornton household. What can I do for you, Mr Rice?'

'Very kind of you, dear lady.' He gave her a smile to match her own. 'Basically, I would like to describe the history of each house from its origins to the present date.'

'That should not be a problem. I have worked for Oswald Thornton since I left school, and I think I can honestly say that there is nothing about Greenfield that I do not know about.'

'In that case, perhaps we should begin at the beginning. By that I mean the oldest part of the house.'

'Obviously, that would be the East Tower.

If you care to follow me, Mr Rice, I will take you there.'

The journalist was only too well aware that he was playing with fire as he permitted Mrs Cameron to lead him along a narrow passageway to a large, iron-studded oaken door. One of the three big houses on his list almost certainly sheltered the treasure, and very probably the killer as well. Indeed, why not surmise further. If one person in the household knew the truth, perhaps all were party to the great secret. It was not outwith the realm of possibility that he, Peter Rice, was walking into oblivion. And no one in the greater world knew where he was or why he might have come to this place. When Mrs Cameron turned the large key in the lock, Rice very genuinely wished he had been less secretive and more inclined to share his theories with others.

'The East Tower, Mr Rice,' the house-keeper announced, pressing the great door inwards to reveal a square, panelled room, not unlike many others he had been in. 'The fireplace is ancient, but the windows were built into the walls during the time of the present Mr Thornton's grandfather. Prior to that it was very much a keep of the old style, erected for defence rather than comfort.'

But it was neither the large fireplace nor

the airy windows that concerned Peter Rice. Having got this far without being overpowered or murdered, he felt a resurgence of his natural confidence and crossed to the middle of the well-scrubbed, but uncarpeted, floor. He had hoped to find a trapdoor, but there was no indication of such a thing anywhere on the oak planking.

'Is there a cellar, Mrs Cameron?' he asked.

'There is a cellar, but not here in the East Tower.' She smiled thinly. 'Unless, of course, there is a secret access in the walls that I know nothing about. They are very thick, you know. Nine feet or more in some places. Numerous people have measured both the inside and the outside of the tower, and have invariably arrived at the conclusion that there may very well be places of concealment hidden in the boulder walls.'

'Surely there must be a wine cellar?' Rice suggested.

'Certainly.' Mrs Cameron permitted him to return to the hallway, then locked the unused keep and invited him to go with her to the living heart of the house. 'Of course, this is nowhere nearly as old as the keep.'

This time a much smaller door in a short passage between the kitchen and the dining room opened onto a flight of stairs. There was a brief resurgence of fear as Rice stared down into the absolute darkness, then Mrs Cameron struck a match, applied it to the wick of a brass lamp on a nearby table and held it out so that it illuminated the descending stairs and the cellar with its many racks.

'As far as I know,' the lady offered, 'this part of the house was built by whoever owned the property prior to the first Mr Thornton. He was the one responsible for making the family fortune in the West Indies.'

'Do you happen to know the name of this early owner?'

'No, I'm afraid I do not, Mr Rice. But I dare say you can find out if it is necessary.'

Since he had told the housekeeper that his brief was to write the history of the large houses from their origins to, Peter Rice was obliged to follow the good Mrs Cameron from room to room, through added wings and more recent additions, even though he was groaning inwardly and desperate to be gone.

Finally, the endurance test was over and he was able to assure her that the *Herald* would give mention to her kindness and assistance. He then set off down the winding road in the direction of Stonewood Mansion.

★ ★ ★

Samuel Keith, confirmed bachelor and retired box manufacturer, was a friendly old fellow, who retained a small staff at Stonewood Mansion. Very much of the old school, he insisted that Peter Rice should take tea before embarking on a tour of the property.

Mr Keith bade Rice to be seated on a settee, pulled the bell cord and took his place on the other side of the long, low table. When the maid did finally put in an appearance, the elderly fellow instructed her to bring tea and scones. Peter Rice assumed that Mr Keith had judged him to be more fond of substantial grub than fancies, and in that he was not wrong.

'A most interesting topic,' Samuel Keith said, while the girl was filling the cups. 'Architectural histories of the big houses in the Vale? Well, I'm sure you'll find plenty to write about. Few of the houses sprang into existence fully formed like Athena from the head of Zeus. Most, and Stonewood is no exception, were built piecemeal over the centuries and exhibit a wide variety of styles, some wonderful, some awful.'

'Do you have any idea how old Stonewood is?' Rice asked.

'The oldest part is about five hundred years and the most recent, the conservatory, was built by me. Between these periods came the main hall, a second storey and the wings; there were all added by various owners throughout the centuries.'

'Your forebears?'

'Good Heavens, no. I'm a poor boy from the Calton, Mr Rice. I started work in the sawmill, then became a porter in the Fruit Market, until I had the bright notion that I could make better and cheaper boxes and pallets. It's all a question of using what knowledge you acquire. I was never a carpenter, but I could get cheap wood nobody else wanted and knew how to nail it together to make a box. In no time at all I had half a dozen men working for me and by my thirtieth birthday I had purchased this place outright.'

'A most inspiring story, Mr Keith,' Peter Rice said warmly. 'You don't mind if I use it?'

'Of course I don't mind. I am proud of my achievements and don't see anything wrong with blowing the bugle.'

Rice lifted his cup, decided that the liquid was still too hot and returned it to its saucer.

'Do you know anything about the original house, Mr Keith?' he enquired.

'Actually, I do. I had a young man working here for several months, and it was his job to create and catalogue a library for me. He did some research on the early history of the property, mainly to do with Bishop Matthew de Glendonwyn and the Western Schism, which was a split within the Roman Catholic Church at the end of the 14th century. To put it briefly, there were two claimants for the role as pope. It was then that Bishop Glendonwyn of Glasgow saw fit to erect a tower away from the Bishop's Palace. One can only guess why he needed a protective shell.'

'Was it incorporated into the house?'

'Of course.' The old man laughed then. 'I find it quite difficult to imagine how they could have entirely removed it. By all accounts, there is more of it under the ground than above it.'

Peter Rice tried hard to keep his rising excitement under control.

'By all accounts?' he echoed.

'Yes, I have never actually seen the legendary subterranean apartment, if apartment is the correct word.'

'Might it be possible to explore it?'

'I am afraid not. When we finish our tea I will show you why.'

Understandably, Samuel Keith was in less of a hurry than his guest. But he did eventually rise from his chair and, with the aid of his walking stick, led the way out into the hall, and from there along a narrow passageway to an open door and the bright day beyond. At that point Peter Rice found himself in an open courtyard, paved with enormous slabs. No two of these were exactly the same size and some seemed over many years to have settled deeper to one side then the other. As a result, it would be only too easy to trip on a raised stone and come quickly to grief.

They crossed the broad yard to a small door set deep in a roughcast and white-washed wall. This door was unlocked, so Mr Keith pressed on it with his stick and it swung open silently.

'Mind your head,' he called over his shoulder as he ducked under the massive lintel. 'Must have been a bit shorter back then.'

Then they were in a square room, the four windowless walls of which had been white-washed, but were otherwise devoid of any decorative pretensions. It was the height, however, that Peter Rice found most surprising. The roof, made entirely of glass panels, was no more than ten or eleven feet from the floor.

'I imagined it to be much higher,' he said.

'And indeed it was.' Samuel Keith laughed at his guest's predictable reaction. 'When I said I couldn't imagine anyone removing the entire edifice I meant exactly that. What a previous owner did do was arrange to have the ancient tower dismantled from the top down until it reached this point, then he had this glass roof put in. He was an artist, I believe, and what you now see is his studio. Speaking personally, I have never been able to decide what to do with the place. I have quite enough rooms already.'

Rice nodded as though he was genuinely interested, when in fact it was the world beneath his boots that intrigued him most.

'You mentioned a considerable cellar, Mr Keith,' he said.

'I suppose you might call it that.' The old man tapped the plank floor with his cane. 'I take the word of those who went before me.'

'And you have never been tempted to have the floor lifted?'

'Good God, no, sir. That is the last thing I want to do.' Samuel Keith closed in on the journalist and asked softly, 'You don't believe in ghosts, do you?'

'Hardly, sir.'

'Which is exactly what I would have said a year or two ago, but now I'm not so sure.'

This turn of events caused the proverbial hackles to rise on Peter Rice's neck.

'Have you seen something strange, Mr

Keith?' he enquired.

'Not see, heard.' The old man was thoughtful for a few moments. 'It started with one of the maids. Even though it was not being used, they sweep this place out regularly and generally keep it free of cobwebs and the like. But one day, about eighteen months ago, the maid who had been sent to dust it down came scurrying across the yard in a bit of a state. She had heard movements, you see, and the sound of someone digging down there, beneath the floorboards.

'Rather than scold the girl, I decided to come over here and listen for myself. After a few minutes I heard what I thought was a rat scratching, until I remembered that the subterranean vault was believed to be more than twenty feet deep. Then the sound became louder and I lost my nerve.'

'Eighteen months ago, you say?' Peter Rice offered. 'But not now?'

'Not for quite some time, sir. To be honest, I don't think it lasted for more than a few days, which makes me suspect that it may have been a wild animal of some sort that had dug its way in. I have no idea how thick the walls would be down below, but I can't think that they would be as stout as the ones on the surface.'

'True,' Peter Rice said, despite his grave misgivings. Neither wild animals nor ghosts posed the kind of threat to his ambitions that he dreaded most. 'It was probably nothing of any great importance.'

Anxious to be on his way to Alder Grange, Peter Rice declined Samuel Keith's kind offer of further refreshment and took his leave, assuring the old man that he would extol the architectural virtues of the property, while omitting to mention entirely any tendency of the house towards the supernatural.

★   ★   ★

Peter Rice had all but given up the idea of investigating the third and final house on his list — Alder Grange — because his experience at Stonewood had left him convinced that something other than the clawing of a wild animal had unnerved the maid and the old man. In short, he harboured a dull dread that he had already been beaten to the treasure.

Yet someone had murdered both Kirchner and Bradwell, so it might well be that the game was still afoot. Thus he found himself trudging up a well-worn buggy path to the large front door of Alder Grange and introducing himself to an elderly butler, who had plainly never encountered a journalist before and was unsure exactly what to do with him.

'If you would kindly wait in the hall, sir,' the old retainer said, 'I will announce you to the Misses Coburn.'

Henrietta, known to her sister as Hettie, and Leonora, who apparently had no abbreviated name, were ladies of small stature both in their late fifties. They received Rice courteously in the drawing room, which appeared much larger than it in fact was by dint of the *trompe-l'oeil* scenery. Every third strip of hand-printed wallpaper was a separate marble column, perfectly shaded and seeming to protrude, while the spaces between depicted a wide bay, in which sailing ships lay at anchor. So perfect was the illusion of depth that Peter Rice would not have been unduly surprised had a figure suddenly appeared from behind a column.

And the coffered ceiling contributed fully to the effect. The plaster grid was smaller and narrower towards the centre, and the baskets of flowers were appropriately smaller, so that the overall impression was that the middle of the ceiling was considerably higher than at the edges. A vault, in fact, or an illusion of one.

As expected, the ladies were delighted by

the prospect of having their house featured in the *Herald*.

'It is a pity that you could not show our décor,' said Hettie, smiling. 'We copied it from an ancient Roman mosaic. They were very fond of such tricks of the eye, you know.'

'Well,' Rice said unashamedly, 'it might be possible to persuade the editor to have it photographed and a realistic engraving made of it.'

'That would be wonderful, Mr Rice,' Leonora twittered. 'We might become fashion-setters yet.'

There was no further talk until the tea ceremony was over, in which Hettie put just the right amount of milk in each cup, Leonora poured the tea into the centre of the cold liquid so as not to risk cracking the eggshell porcelain, and Hettie relinquished her control of the milk jug to take command of the silver sugar-bowl.

'I am led to understand, ladies,' Rice began, 'that all of the large houses in the Vale began life as relatively simple keeps, or towers, Alder Grange being no exception. Is that the case?'

'It most certainly is,' Leonora replied, then deferred to her sister for her to provide more information.

'It dates from before the time of Mary

Queen of Scots,' Hettie added. 'But I don't believe it was ever called upon to serve as a fortress. The men of the Vale were supporters of Murray against Mary, so I suppose had she triumphed instead of him the tower might have known a siege.'

Anxious to avoid a full-blown lecture on sixteenth century history, Peter Rice quickly changed the subject.

'Is the tower still extant?' he enquired.

'Indeed it is.' This from Leonora. 'Alder Grange is the only house to incorporate the original keep into the facade. You may not have noticed, Mr Rice, but that simple structure has been duplicated on the east wing. The frontage appears perfectly symmetrical, which I suppose it is, but one wing is fully two or more centuries older than the other.'

'So it is still in use?'

'As our library, Mr Rice. When you are ready to view it, our butler, Isam, will take you there.'

'But I am sure there must be a great deal you want to hear before that,' Hettie suggested. 'Leonora and I are very much in love with Alder Grange. We have made it our lifetimes' study.'

'In that case, you will save me a great deal of research, ladies.' Peter Rice dug out his notebook and pencil, but they were merely for effect. If the place had potential after all, anything they had to tell him would be absorbed and remembered word for word. If not, it would be instantly forgotten and consigned to the bin of unnecessary thoughts. 'Now, for how long has the property been in your family?'

'We know exactly how long, Mr Rice,' Hettie said, glancing at Leonora and receiving a brief nod of approval, 'but we are less certain about its earlier history.'

'There is the book, Hettie dear,' Leonora advised.

'Yes, the book, but I fear it may not be reliable. I get the impression that there is an element of imagination in the telling.'

'I agree, but fanciful or not, I am sure that the core of the account is true.'

If they had intended to drive Peter Rice to distraction they could not have made a more thorough job of it.

'Book?' he said, trying to sound as nonchalant as possible.

'Yes,' Hettie replied politely. 'Father found it in an old writing desk. It had been deliberately hidden below the false base of a drawer. Father, you see, was very persistent. Once he got it into his head that there must be a secret compartment in the desk he would not let up until he found it.'

'Do you know what it contained?'

'Oh yes,' Leonora contributed, 'but you may see it yourself, Mr Rice. We keep it in the tower library. It is simply known as the Old Book.'

'In the meantime,' said Hettie, 'would you care to hear our own family's connection with Alder Grange?'

'Very much, Miss Coburn.' In saying this, Rice was being perfectly truthful. It was possible that the mysterious book held early information about the treasure; anything that had happened to the treasure had taken place in the time the Coburns had lived at the Grange. And that period most certainly covered the loss of at least one box into the river. But of course all that depended on Alder Grange being the true depository of the hoard. The whole thing might well be nothing more than a cruel coincidence. 'Do you know approximately when the Coburns acquired the house?'

'Not approximately, Mr Rice,' Leonora replied. 'Exactly. It was June 15, 1748. The date is carved into the lintel above the front door. The owner at that time was Jasper Morrison, our great-grandfather. It was he who changed the name of the property to Alder Grange.

'He died in 1779, and the property fell to his daughter, Wilhemina Morrison, our grandmother, who married Rupert Coburn, owner of the nearby cut nail mill.

'Wilhemina died in 1814, Rupert having predeceased her, and the property then fell to their only son, Martin, our father, who passed away in 1847, leaving a wife, Catherine, and us. Mother has since joined him, so we are now the joint mistresses of Alder Grange, for good or ill.'

'Which can be something of a worry at times,' Hettie added. 'There is the family mausoleum, for example. It was built by Jasper Morrison shortly after he acquired the house.'

Peter Rice was confused.

'Is it full?' he asked, and immediately felt stupid.

'Not full, Mr Rice, deteriorating. We noticed some time ago that the iron gate no longer fitted properly. Now a builder has informed us that the tomb may be in danger of subsiding.'

'Yes,' Leonora put in, 'the subsidence is being caused by an underground stream, you see. There was a great deal of rain last winter and it seems that at least one of the floor slabs fell into the watercourse. It may be that we will have to build a new mausoleum and

275

transfer our forebears to that.'

But Peter Rice was only vaguely conscious of what she was saying. His mind was full of thoughts of ancient towers with deep cellars that were possibly dungeons, the sound of exploratory digging in the case of Stonewood Mansion and very probably the others too. His theorizing raced on to flooded underground watercourses that could provide access routes for anyone adventurous enough to risk their lives by the light of a Davy lamp or a Geordie lamp; *Spéléologie* was how intrepid French explorers called such underground work — and undermining by water was known to weaken the floors of such medieval cellars to the extent that they would collapse in part or in full. Was this the fate of the box the dredger had scooped up from the silt at Pointhouse? Had it and its companions been stored in a place like that, perhaps for many years, before the power of incessant subterranean water had swept away all the rocks and clay beneath the ancient stones? He could well imagine those old slabs dropping into the tumbling underground rivers, taking with them sealed boxes that would then be swept along and downwards into the River Kelvin, and from there to the Clyde at Pointhouse. Perhaps by then sufficient water would have seeped into the chests to cause

276

them to sink until retrieved by the dredger. In a few short seconds he had persuaded himself that this was how it had happened, and that he was the only one alive who knew the truth.

Before Rice could think of further questions, Miss Hettie gave her silver bell a couple of quick rings, causing the party to wait in silence until Isam pressed open the double door and stood on the threshold awaiting instructions.

'Take Mr Rice to the library, Isam,' Miss Hettie said. 'Furnish him with the Old Book and anything else he may require.'

★ ★ ★

Shortly thereafter, armed with the information he required, Peter Rice was once more on the path above the gorge when a noise claimed his attention.

At first he was sure that it was just a combination of his imagination and the echo of his own footsteps. When he stopped walking, however, the other footfalls did not. And that was when panic set in.

Whatever was pursuing him was not directly in his wake. More likely it was level with him, matching him step for step, but hidden from sight by the dense trees. He glanced round to his right and left, but saw nothing that could be creating the sounds of snapping twigs and thudding boots then, surrendering to blind panic, he tumbled forth, headlong and with arms flailing.

His thoughts were in complete disarray. In the five or so minutes after he left Alder Grange he had been able to think clearly, even though he was unable to decide which of the properties was most likely to house the secreted boxes, but now he was beyond reasoning. He could think only of the painted face of the monster as he stumbled through the woods, impacting with one tree and being thrown against another. He tripped over flesh-ripping brambles and clambered madly to his feet once more, while all the time the pounding of a determined, unrelenting predator came ever louder.

Then there was nothing beneath his feet. He was moving his legs, but they failed to make contact with solid ground until a tooth-jarring impact brought it home to him that he had run blindly over the edge of the near-vertical gully. But his unintentional descent was not over. What he had landed on was merely a slimy, moss-covered outcrop, so that almost immediately he found himself again in freefall until an even greater shock swept over him in the form of the cold, tumbling waters of the River Kelvin. Then he was being swept along the coarse gravel bed, unable to get to his feet, unable to breathe and terrifyingly aware that these were the last few seconds of his life.

High above, Jaguar Claw, High Priest of the Cloud People, watched in vain for some sign that his prey had survived. Reluctantly, for once again he had been denied his sacrifice to the gods for the soul of King Pezelao, he turned away and began his trek back to that infernal place from which he was utterly determined to escape.

12

Jaguar Claw felt despair; day by day, his awareness of his loathsome condition slipped away and became a hazy world of nebulous figures that came and went. Sometimes the figures spoke to him without receiving an answer. On other occasions, because his task was incomplete, he strove for sufficient lucidity to hold a meaningful conversation with these foreigners, or to drive his own buggy, or rip the living heart from a human being. When he did this he knew exactly what he was doing and why.

The journalist, Rice, was no great loss. His heart would have been a paltry affair, little more than an insult to the King, yet it should have been taken because he was another who sought to possess the sacred goods.

The next sacrifice, then, had to be a truly magnificent one, a heart that would satisfy the gods and guarantee a safe journey for Pezelao.

★　★　★

Superintendent Henry Jarrett rose from his chair and quickly left the office at Charlie

Grant's insistence that this was something he ought to hear.

The man in the interview room was ashen grey, his complexion being only a few shades lighter than the cheap, colourless suit they had provided him with at the Royal Infirmary. His bandaged head gave him an unfortunate comic appearance. His left hand was also bound and he was clearly protecting it with his right.

'Good lord, Mr Rice,' Jarrett said. 'You've been in the wars.'

'I've been to hell and out the other side, if that's what you mean, Superintendent.' Rice grimaced and hugged his injured extremity. 'They say I was lucky not to have bashed my brains in. I hit my head on a rock, broke two fingers, swallowed half a river and was saturated to the marrow. I still don't know how I managed to get out of the water, and I don't remember getting to the Royal.'

'The local police took you there,' Charlie Grant offered.

'Then I owe them my life.'

'Who paid for your treatment?'

'I believe they found out who I was from my notebook and got in touch with Mr McGovern, who very kindly paid the costs — so he is not such a bad fellow after all.'

'Or he thinks you've got a good story for

him,' Charlie suggested.

'Yes, I suppose that might be closer to the truth.'

'I would say you have a story for us too,' Jarrett said, 'and we take priority.'

'I won't argue with that, Superintendent. I was stupid, but all that's behind me now. I came within a hair's breadth of being murdered.'

Jarrett nodded approvingly.

'Perhaps you should begin at the beginning, Mr Rice,' he advised. 'Don't leave anything out, because there is always the possibility that you may have information pertinent to a case in hand.'

Rice frowned as he reviewed the sequence of events in his mind.

'Well,' he said, 'I suppose it started with a sheaf of papers handed down by my mother's grandfather, Lucius Holman, who worked as a warder in the Garngad Insane Asylum. During his time there he became acquainted with an inmate by the name of Tobias Fisher, who claimed to have stolen a great fortune and hidden it somewhere on his estate. Fisher also admitted to Holman that he had clubbed to death his manservant because he was a witness to the theft.

'Unfortunately, Lucius Holman's account was almost entirely bereft of good, hard facts, so no one could be sure whether his story was just the kind of wild ravings you would get in a place like that. There was no clear idea of exactly what he had stolen or where he had concealed it, which meant that there was nowhere to start. He didn't even give the name of his estate. Holman, however, noted that the governor of the asylum, Jasper Morrison, would have a record of where Fisher had been seized by the stewards and the reason for it. As it turned out, this was pivotal to the whole story.

'Anyway, one fact Fisher emphasized time and again was that his 'treasure' as he called it was concealed in eight boxes. But as for the servant he said he had murdered, there was no name given and no indication of where the body had been concealed.

'All in all the account meant little or nothing to me, being extremely short on substance. Every now and again I would read through it, though, searching for some little detail I had overlooked, but it was always the same thin account. Then a year or so ago I happened upon Dr Hamilton's lecture at the Mechanics Institute. He was talking about a century-old murder victim and the strange design on the club used to kill him. You may believe me, gentlemen, when I say that from that very moment I have been obsessed with finding Tobias Fisher's hidden hoard. It was no longer a madman's ravings. I had to find those boxes, no matter what they contained.'

'Out of interest,' Henry Jarrett said at this point, 'how much did you tell Jake McGovern?'

'Nothing.'

'Are you saying that his treatment of the jade mask picture was a pure coincidence?'

'I'm not sure that anything Mr McGovern does can be termed pure, but he certainly didn't know about the treasure boxes, and still doesn't as far as I know.'

'But he must think you're about to deliver something big?'

'Let's say I hinted at a sensational story along those lines.'

Jarrett gave this a few moments' thought, then asked, 'How did you get in touch with Johannes Kirchner and Elisha Bradwell?'

Rice smiled thinly.

'I've been a newspaper man for a long time,' he said. 'I have contacts in every big hotel in the city, so I get to hear about any famous, strange or otherwise interesting person as soon as they sign in.'

'Moira Pearce, Victoria Hotel?'

'Precisely. A young lady with an eye for a few bob.' Rice shrugged. 'I suppose in her position I would do the same. Anyway, she told me how Bradwell had almost no luggage, and devoted himself to keeping an eye on the Architectural Records office. She also obtained a page of his notebook for me with the name of Kirchner and the boarding house he was living in.

'Then it was just a matter of calling upon Mrs Hyslop at 94 Benton Mews, near the Great Western Road, and letting her know that I was doing a piece on local boarding-houses. Some of these ladies will talk the back legs off a horse if you give them half a chance.'

'So she told you about Kirchner?'

'Everything. If you ask me the dainty Mrs Hyslop had been going through his belongings with a fine tooth-comb.'

Jarrett and Grant both knew full well that there was something big yet to come, something Peter Rice was deliberately holding back. They also knew that pushing him could have an adverse effect, so no matter how anxious they were to find out what he knew about the killer, there was nothing else for it but to tread softly.

'Why did you supply Kirchner and Bradwell with the information you got from Dr Hamilton's laboratory?' the superintendent asked in a tone that suggested it didn't really matter.

'It wasn't like that,' Rice admitted. 'I didn't know how much they knew and that was concerning me somewhat. I decided to approach them in my role as a journalist, but Elisha Bradwell didn't take kindly to that. He was annoyed by the possibility of publicity, and even threatened to take action against me if I violated his privacy. Johannes Kirchner was an entirely different character. He saw a chance to turn the tables and offered me a considerable sum of money if I obtained certain information for him.'

'The burial site of the servant?' Charlie Grant asked.

'Exactly, Inspector. Kirchner knew from the first moment we met that I wasn't interested in interviewing him. He suggested that as a newspaperman I had a way of getting facts that might be denied to the ordinary man. He even went as far as to say that he could hire a common burglar, except that he wouldn't know what to look for.

'Anyway, as you know, I found out what he wanted and passed it on to him. The deal was quite simply that he would pay me five thousand pounds if, and only if, the information led him to the treasure. I can see how it might make me seem a bit gullible, but I had no choice but to play it his way.

'Not being entirely simple, I tailed

286

Kirchner that evening, knowing that the first thing he would do was make his way to the place. It didn't take long for me to realize that Bradwell's modus operandi was different from Kirchner's. He preferred to let the opposition do the work, then follow him and see what he was up to. I was lucky that Bradwell didn't see me, so I was able to keep an eye on both of them.'

Casually, almost nonchalantly, Henry Jarrett asked, 'You saw more than that, Mr Rice, didn't you? There is no need to worry about getting into trouble, because we know you didn't kill anyone.'

'Look at it this way,' Charlie Grant put in. 'The sooner we get this man behind bars the sooner you will be able to sleep in peace.'

'And there will be no charge of withholding information?'

'None at all. You can fairly claim to have been unwell and not able to come forward until now.'

'Very well.' Peter Rice licked his lips nervously. 'I saw a dreadful thing. I saw a monster rip out a man's heart.'

'Did you see the killer's face?' Jarrett asked, relieved that it was going so smoothly. He had expected a considerable amount of wheedling.

'Yes, he looked straight at me, so naturally I

287

thought he would come after me.'

'Describe him.'

'Taller than average, thin and with coloured streaks on his face and body.'

'Did you recognize him?'

'No. As a matter of fact, I'm not sure that I would know even a familiar face if it was smeared with paint.' Rice hugged his aching hand and looked for all the world like a beaten man. 'At that moment I decided to have nothing more to do with the whole affair. It was only when you told me that Kirchner and Bradwell were dead that I dared to think about the possibility of actually pulling it off. Thanks to Kirchner's request for the site of the old grave I now knew as much as anyone and more than most.

'It was clear that Fisher could only have chased the manservant so far, so it was quite easy to narrow the hiding place of the boxes down to one of three properties: Greenfield House, Stonewood Mansion and Alder Grange. I inveigled my way into each and had just left Alder Grange when I became aware that I was being followed. I don't recall much after that except waking up in the Royal Infirmary.'

Jarrett leaned back, folded his arms and considered the man's story.

'Where are the boxes, Mr Rice,' he asked.

'I'm not completely certain.'

'Where do you think they are?'

Peter Rice squirmed in his chair as he desperately sought to hold on to that last piece of information. But it was no use. The Fates had snatched him out of the clutches of a blood-thirsty monster and given him a chance for life. He wouldn't be that lucky, or that deserving again.

'Alder Grange,' he said softly. 'The founder of the present dynasty was one Jasper Morrison, the governor of the Garngad Lunatic Asylum. It is too much of a coincidence that a man who knew Fisher's story should buy his house when he died. I wouldn't even be surprised if Fisher's death was less than absolutely natural.'

'Whether it was or it wasn't is of no interest to us after all this time. He most certainly had nothing to do with the recent killings.' Jarrett rose to his feet. 'One final thing, Mr Rice. Are you acquainted with a man called Gideon Mallam?'

Rice shook his head.

'Sorry, Superintendent,' he said. 'I meet a lot of people, but I'm sure I've never had the pleasure.'

'I frankly doubt if you could call it that,' said the superintendent. 'Now, if you will excuse me I have matters to attend to. I would like you to wrack your brains and let Inspector Grant have any other little facts you might suddenly recall.'

'Certainly, Superintendent,' Peter Rice said, adding, 'If you recall, you did promise to let me have the whole story when it was all wrapped up. Does that still apply? It is probably all I'm going to get out of this.'

Jarrett paused at the doorway.

'It applies,' he confirmed. 'You deserve at least that much for your trials and tribulations.'

★ ★ ★

When Superintendent Henry Jarrett left headquarters it was not through the front door as usual, but down the iron staircase that led to the yard. From his small, but neat living quarters above the stables PC Jamieson saw the boss's descent, cursed mildly because he then half-expected his free afternoon to go the way of all things, then hurried down to meet Jarrett.

'We're out and about, Superintendent?' the driver observed.

'We are indeed, Jamieson. I want you to take me to Evan Youngson & Company in St. Enoch Square. They are the shipping and commission agent for the Red Anchor Line.

After that you can take me home.'

'I have always found that to be the best solution when the going gets tough,' PC Jamieson stated, as he brought Domino to the wagonette. 'Run away. Or in this instance, sail away.'

'I am neither running nor sailing, my man,' Jarrett corrected. 'I am testing a theory. So I suggest you keep your homespun philosophy for your companions on tonight's surveillance operation.'

'We are out tonight again?'

'Tonight and every night until Mallam makes a move.'

★ ★ ★

Clement Broadhurst of Evan Youngson & Company was quite evidently not in the habit of being visited by the police, and certainly not a senior officer of Jarrett's calibre.

'Mr Mallam?' he repeated in answer to the superintendent's question. 'I'm sorry, sir, but I am not at liberty to divulge such information.'

'Mr Broadhurst,' Henry Jarrett said calmly, 'you are neither a doctor nor a priest, so you are bound by no oath of secrecy. I want to know the circumstances of Mr Mallam's most recent visit to Central America, and I expect you to co-operate fully.'

Such resistance as Broadhurst could summon up now collapsed and he dabbed his perspiring forehead with a large linen handkerchief.

'Mr Mallam's last visit was in 1861,' he said, flicking through the pages of a large ledger. 'I remember that because he is due to sail in just over three weeks from now. I took the booking myself.'

'Tell me about such sailings, Mr Broadhurst,' Jarrett invited. 'Their frequency, for example, and how many passengers you might carry.'

'Well, sailings are monthly for the West Indies and Central America, Superintendent. The present Red Anchor Line vessels are the *Mary Lynn* and the *Princess Adeline*. These are primarily merchant ships, of course. Unlike the Canadian and Australian emigrant ships, there is no steerage and accommodation is limited to eight cabins.'

'Did Mr Mallam travel alone?'

'Oh yes. Single cabin.'

Jarrett reached across the desk and took the red leather ledger from Mr Broadhurst, who relinquished it without so much as a whimper.

'If it is all right with you, sir,' Henry Jarrett said, 'I will take this with me. You will have it back in a day or so.'

'Dear me. Is that necessary?'

'Absolutely.' Jarrett smiled at him. 'And it might be a good idea for me to take the passenger lists for '60 and '62, if you don't mind.'

'But Mr Mallam didn't sail in those years.'

'No, I know, but I would like them anyway.'

★ ★ ★

Shortly before eight o'clock that evening a Hansom cab turned into Clairemont Drive, proceeded along the cul-de-sac and drew up in front of Hillview Villa. By then it was exactly on the hour.

Immediately, the front door of the house opened and Gideon Mallam descended the dozen or so steps at speed and took his place within the vehicle. The Hansom then wheeled around and set off back the way it had come. PC Jamieson, suitably attired in civilian garb, encouraged Domino forward, but endeavoured to keep a decent distance between the black van and its quarry.

Given the roads to themselves, the Hansom and the van could have reached St Vincent Street in fifteen minutes or so, but it was a good half an hour before the gondola suddenly drew to a halt. Then Mallam jumped out and hurried down Bottle Lane in the direction of West George Street.

'Right, Russell,' DC Williamson shouted, 'you and PC Akins get after him. Chapman and I will cut him off in West George Street.'

As soon as the detective and the uniformed officer were out and running, PC Jamieson drove Domino into a gallop, spun left into George Square, then left again into West George Street. DC Williamson, who was holding the van doors half open, threw them wide and leapt out, closely followed by Walter Chapman. They was just in time to meet DC Russell as he emerged from Bottle Lane.

'Where the bloody hell is he?' Williamson demanded of no one in particular. 'Where did he go, Russell?'

'No idea. I didn't see him,' DC Russell said, adding, 'Should we let Superintendent Jarrett know?'

No one answered. They merely stared at him until he saw the foolishness of his remark.

13

The sun was shining, Albert Sweetman was still absent, kedgeree was one of Henry Jarrett's favourite breakfasts and all was well with the world. He nodded amiably to Wilbur McConnell, noted that Elliot Stainer was still studiously avoiding him, then took his place at his usual table and checked his silver hunter for the third time since he woke.

That was when Elsie Maitland appeared at the doorway to the dining room, gave him a small wave by way of a warning, and hurried over to his table.

'Sorry to interrupt you, Superintendent,' she whispered, 'but your police driver is outside. I understand that you are required rather urgently.'

★ ★ ★

Although PC Jamieson had only managed to grab a few hours' sleep, what with one thing and another, he was his usual breezy self as he guided Domino around lesser vehicles and generally showed the rest of the road users how to drive. Those who refused to yield to his innate superiority received an earful and wave of the whip.

'I trust you wouldn't use that thing,' Jarrett observed.

Jamieson was offended to the quick.

'Not on the horse, sir,' he said. 'Never on Domino. A crack above the head is all that's needed.'

'I was talking about other drivers.'

'Bugger them, sir.'

Inspector Charlie Grant was waiting on the pavement and Sergeant Tommy Quinn stood by the sliding door to the former Foreign Merchandise warehouse in Clyde Lane. Both looked as though they had dressed quickly and come away without breakfast. Nearby, DCs Williamson and Russell were even worse, and Acting DC Chapman looked positively ill. None had been home since early the previous morning.

'At the risk of appearing facetious, good morning, sir,' Grant offered. 'Has PC Jamieson filled you in?'

'As much as I need to know, Inspector, and more than I would prefer to know. Is it positive?'

'Sergeant Quinn and I both saw him in headquarters, sir. It's Gideon Mallam all right.'

Accompanied by Grant and Quinn, Henry

Jarrett crossed the empty, echoing building to the place where Dr Hamilton was waiting by the sheet-covered corpse.

'Same as before, Superintendent,' Hamilton said casually. 'Killed and mutilated right here.'

'Who discovered the body?'

'A dosser. Came in here out of the cold, found the body, and reported it to the beat man. Unfortunately, he ran off before the constable could detain him, so we don't know if he is away with any of Mallam's possessions.'

'Hardly important now. Any sign of a struggle?'

'None whatsoever. He must have arrived here with the killer and been struck down when his attention was directed elsewhere.' Hamilton reached down to the pile of clothes that had been Mallam's garments in life and lifted a silver-topped cane. This he drew open to reveal an eighteen-inch-long blade of triangular section. 'Good quality item. This would send any robber fleeing.'

'Except that he had no chance to draw it.'

'Or no reason to. Whatever the killer told these men was sufficient to make them careless. And I think we all know what that must have been.'

Jarrett nodded, but his expression warned

297

that there were uniforms present who were not party to what had been going on.

'I think the sooner you get him out of here the better,' the superintendent said softly.

'The blood wagon has been sent for, Superintendent.'

Tommy Quinn glanced at Charlie Grant and received a nod. Now would be as good a time as any, if there was such a thing.

'Superintendent Jarrett,' he said, 'the men were in pursuit of Mallam but lost him in George Square. He must have known they were behind him.'

Jarrett nodded grimly.

'PC Jamieson told me about the slip,' he said. 'Don't worry about it, Sergeant. And you can tell them that we are all equally to blame.'

'But how can you — ?'

'How can I be to blame? Because I knew last night that Gideon Mallam was not the killer. My mistake was in hoping that nothing would happen before morning, so we could get the whole thing wrapped up without another death.'

Even Charlie Grant, long experienced though he was, stared at Jarrett as though unable to believe his ears.

'How could you possibly find that out?' he asked. 'You were sure of Mallam's guilt. We all were.'

'Sergeant Quinn wasn't, and that's what started me thinking. When I left here yesterday I called in at the office of the shipping agent for the Red Anchor Line and took possession of the passenger lists for the last three years.' Jarrett produced a paper fold from his coat pocket. 'It took me all evening and a couple of the wee small hours to find this. Nigel Greenaway sailed for Central America in February 1860 and returned just six weeks ago.'

Now it was Tommy Quinn's turn to reflect astonishment.

'But he seemed so pleasant,' he breathed. 'When we talked to him he was just like a harmless academic whose knowledge came from books.'

'I think you'll find that his knowledge comes from more than mere books, Sergeant. Whatever he became involved in when he was out there turned him into what he is.'

'Surely it could all be completely harmless?' Charlie Grant suggested. 'A coincidence, perhaps?'

'How far are you prepared to take coincidences, Inspector?' said Jarrett, handing him the sheet. 'Have a look at the passenger list.'

Frowning, Charlie Grant scanned the names Jarrett had penned in his neat hand.

'Johannes Kirchner,' he said at length.

'Precisely. Of course, it doesn't prove that Greenaway and Kirchner became acquainted on the voyage, but the other six are either married ladies or merchants.' Jarrett turned then to Tommy Quinn. 'You call on Greenaway at the university, Sergeant. Take Williamson and Russell with you. And don't argue with me. Subduing a madman is not the same as putting restrainers on a burglar.'

'I was only going to say that he is not likely to be there at this time of the day.'

'Then find out where he lives and run him to ground. In the meantime, Inspector Grant and I are going to cover the third possibility, namely Alder Grange. I am guessing that Peter Rice is correct in believing that the other boxes are hidden there, and that they are the reason for the murders. That being the case, Greenaway cannot have taken possession of the rest of the stuff, or he would not still be killing the opposition. Sooner or later he is going to have to put in an appearance. I hope it will be sooner.'

'If that is the real reason for the murders, sir.'

'Sergeant Quinn, I am not able to imagine any other reason, so unless you can think of one you have your orders. See to them.'

★ ★ ★

Not a great deal was stirring in the corridors of the university on the High Street when Tommy Quinn and his team arrived. The first port of call was Greenaway's office, but that was locked, so they tried all of the other offices on that corridor until they found one that was open and occupied.

Dr Prentiss was more annoyed than surprised. He removed his pince-nez and glared at Tommy Quinn until the latter produced his brass badge.

'How exactly can I help you?' Prentiss asked. It was civil, but scarcely friendly.

'Professor Greenaway,' Tommy said.

'What about him?'

'Do you happen to know where he is?'

'God alone knows. What has he done, anyway?'

'I'm afraid I can't divulge that, sir.'

'No matter.' Prentiss clipped his glasses back on the bridge of his thin nose. 'Whatever it is, I can't say I am surprised.'

'Really? Why is that?'

'Because the man has become very peculiar, that's why not. Used to be the nicest individual you could wish to meet, but ever since his trip abroad he has turned decidedly funny. Sometimes he seems quite normal, but on other occasions he doesn't reply when spoken to.'

'Do you know where he lives?'

'I think so.' Prentiss reached for his large Stamford diary and flipped open the cover. 'Here you are. 27 Derby Terrace.'

★ ★ ★

The lady who opened the door would have been a very strange creature indeed had she not reflected surprise at the sight of two grown men occupying her top step. Nor did the news that they were detectives do much to lessen her concern. Being the only one with any real experience of the ribbons, DC Russell again remained on the driving bench of the black van.

'Mrs Nichols,' the lady said when Quinn and Williams were inside the hallway and the door to the nosey world was closed once more. 'I am Professor Greenaway's housekeeper. How may I help you?'

'Is your employer at home?' Tommy Quinn asked.

'No.' The look of concern on her face was quite genuine. 'The Professor left an hour ago. Presumably he is at the university.'

'No, he isn't there.'

'Then I have no idea where he may have gone.'

'Tell me, Mrs Nichols,' Tommy Quinn said,

'does Professor Greenaway have a special room, one that only he uses?'

'Only his bedroom, sir. Neither I nor the maid-of-all-work are allowed to tidy it. In fact, we are not even supposed to enter it.'

'Perhaps you would like to enter it now.'

'Oh, I don't know, sir. I mean, orders are orders.'

'I am afraid this matter supersedes orders, Mrs Nichols. You have a key?'

'Yes, of course.' She led the way upstairs and paused in front of a large, black-enamelled door while she sorted through the numerous keys on her belt ring before selecting the right one. 'I'm afraid it might not be quite what you expect.'

Dozens of cold candles in a wide variety of holders covered almost every horizontal surface. These would be the only source of light. The gas lamps on the walls were shorn of their glass covers and mantles and there were no oil lamps, standing or otherwise.

And no furniture — only colourful blankets and mats.

'Unusual,' Sergeant Quinn observed.

'He had men dismantle the bed and store it away in a box room,' Mrs Nichols said softly, as though she was somehow responsible and consequently ashamed. 'He sleeps on mats on the floor.'

'How long has this been going on?'

'Only since he spent time abroad. Ever since he came back he has been different. It changed him. He doesn't speak much now, and sometimes he won't eat.'

But Sergeant Quinn was only half listening to what the housekeeper had to say. A small volume placed reverently in the bowl decorated with the image of a reclining demon-faced being had caught his attention. *MacAusland: Cave Systems Of The Kelvin Valley.* He flicked through the volume and laid it back where it seemingly belonged.

'Now we know how he gained underground access to the big houses,' he remarked. 'Mad or not, he must have all the guts in the world.'

Tommy Quinn crossed to a hanging blanket, stood before it for a few moments, then reached out and drew it aside. The only thing in the alcove was an iron-bound camphorwood box with oval handles.

'When did he bring this home?'

'Yesterday,' the housekeeper said softly. 'He told me there were others, but he could only get one on the dog cart at a time.'

'In that case we'll intrude no further, Mrs Nichols.' Quinn gestured to Williamson and made for the door. 'Your assistance has been invaluable.'

At Alder Grange, the Misses Coburn were anything but put out by the arrival of three detectives and a uniformed officer. In fact, they treated it as something of a show staged entirely for their benefit. In contrast to this reaction their butler, Isam, seemed rather anxious, but held his peace because he knew his place.

In the library, located precisely in front of the medieval fireplace, a large slab lay on the floor. Both the Holman account and the Old Book discovered by the ladies' father called this the Bishop's Stone; it was fully six feet in length and three in width. What was not known, however, was its thickness.

They had brought with them four jemmies, two sledgehammers, a couple of bullseye lamps and an assortment of ropes. Acting DC Walter Chapman was about to find out what it meant to be young and fit and subordinate.

He was also lucky. While he was holding the largest crowbar and wondering what he was supposed to do with it, the wagonette arrived and their numbers were dramatically increased.

'Williamson and Russell,' Superintendent Jarrett instructed, 'give Chapman and the officer a hand to lift that slab.'

'It's Greenaway all right,' Tommy Quinn told Jarrett and Grant in low tones. 'We think he is either here already or on his way.'

'How can you be certain about that?' asked Jarrett.

'He already has one of the boxes and he is after the other six.'

'Right,' the superintendent said to all and sundry, 'let's get a move on. I want that slab lifted or slid aside.'

Centuries of dust and grit made it virtually impossible to gain purchase on any vertical edge of the large stone, but persistence finally paid off and the curved horns of one of the jemmies eventually managed to bite into the red sandstone. Immediately, all four crowbars were concentrated on that one spot and the slab slowly, but definitely, started to rise from its bed. When it was three or so inches proud of the recess Tommy Quinn shoved the head of a sledgehammer beneath it to keep it there. That freed up the jemmies to worry at one of the long sides.

'I don't believe for a single moment that they went through all this trouble every time they wanted to throw some poor unfortunate into the bottle dungeon,' Jarrett said to Charlie Grant.

'I was thinking the same thing, sir,' the inspector agreed. 'According to Rice, the

Holman account states that Fisher and his manservant moved the Bishop's Stone themselves.'

'Right,' Superintendent Henry Jarrett announced and they all turned their faces towards him. 'Something is wrong. Two men are known to have moved this slab, so there has to be some other way.'

It was Walter Chapman who arrived at the only possible solution.

'It's balanced, Superintendent,' he said. 'No two men in the world could lift this thing out. It has to swivel on a shaft.'

'With some way of keeping it locked so that no one could accidentally step on it,' Tommy Quinn added.

Since there were no grooves on the adjacent stones that could have housed slip bolts or the like, Henry Jarrett closed in on the large fireplace and began to examine the various iron fittings. The purposes for most of them were self-evident, but a couple of stout rings were attached to thick rods that disappeared into the walls of the great fireplace and did not appear to have anything to do with roasting meat or suspending pots. In one case the rod was almost entirely buried in the stone; the other was protruding a full foot.

'Better stand aside, gentlemen,' he announced

and they complied.

At first neither ring would budge. It seemed reasonable to assume that the depressed ring ought to be pulled and the distended one pushed, but it was also possible that in the hundred and twenty years since Fisher had secreted the boxes a combination of rust and dirt had rendered them immovable by normal means.

'Let me try this,' Sergeant Quinn said, lifting one of the sledgehammers. 'It shouldn't take much more than a tap.'

It took three. On the third light blow the projecting bar slid into the hole in the stone as far as the ring. As this was happening, the other rod emerged its full length and the sandstone slab swivelled on a hidden axle until it stood vertically. It was clear that a small difference in the weight of the sides permitted gravity to do the work, while at the same time allowing the stone to be returned to the closed, horizontal position with very little human effort at all.

The bottle dungeon was a black, impenetrable pit. The uniformed constable raised the chimneys on the bullseye lamps, applied a match to the trimmed wicks, lowered the cases over the flames and held up one of the items for anyone who chose to accept it. Walter Chapman took him up on it and their combined lamps flooded the grim vault with flickering yellow light.

No humans occupied the cold pit, alive or dead, but the six remaining boxes could be seen casting their solid shadows against the grey boulder wall. Where a seventh box might have rested, however, was a black gash in the cobblestone floor.

'Just as Rice said,' Charlie Grant offered. 'The base of the chamber has started to drop into an underground watercourse.'

'Right,' Jarrett agreed, 'which is why Greenaway is starting to move them out.'

Just then, Acting DC Chapman turned his lamp onto another dark patch on the opposite wall.

'Superintendent,' he said, 'I think that's how he gets in.'

'He is either very determined,' Jarrett observed, 'or completely mad.'

'I think we have already established that.'

Tommy Quinn lifted one of the rope coils and began to tie it tightly around his chest into the armpits. 'Stout lads wanted to lower me, and more important bring me up again,' he said.

Nobody argued with him or offered to take his place. Nor, strictly speaking, should they have. Quinn was the youngest and presumably the fittest of the senior officers, so it would naturally befall him to undertake anything energetic or hazardous. He was also superior to the DCs and the uniformed man, and as such would not order them to do anything that he would not willingly undertake himself.

Quinn dropped another coil of rope onto the cobblestone floor of the vault, then took possession of one of the bullseye lamps and seated himself at the edge of the hole, while the constables gathered up the slack and braced themselves. When they were ready, he launched himself into mid-air and rotated slowly while the natural twist of the rope unwound itself. Little by little he was lowered into the prison until his feet just touched the cobbles and no more. Only when he felt that the remainder of the floor was quite firm was enough of the rope paid out to allow him to move freely around the gloomy and forbidding chamber.

He laid down the lamp and proceeded to tie the boxes together by threading the spare rope through the oval handles and forming what in his opinion were fairly secure knots. When he had made a daisy-chain of the six boxes and discovered that he had a good bit of rope left, he used that up by threading it back through the handles, thus doubling the strength of the links.

But no sooner had he finished this than his attention was directed to the access hole in the far wall by a hoarse whisper from above. What had previously been a dark and lifeless tunnel was now filled by an orange glow that grew stronger by the second.

Immediately, he grabbed up the light and thumbed the metal shield over the frosted lens and the dungeon fell into darkness.

One minute passed, then two, before the glowing mesh tube of a Davy lamp appeared at the entrance to the man-made cave and a thin man, already familiar to Tommy Quinn, crouched and entered the dungeon. Up above, the other bullseye torch had been similarly masked, but the new arrival must have seen the dark rectangular hole, for he instantly swung the Davy lamp right and left in search of unwanted intruders. When the light fell on the immobile shape of Tommy Quinn, Greenaway let out a howl of anger.

His next act was entirely predetermined. No matter how dangerous the situation, or how much the odds were stacked against him, he could not flee and leave the precious grave goods of Pezelao to these savages. There was nowhere he could hide from the gods, and no excuse would quell their wrath.

The razor-sharp obsidian dagger had been drilled through the hilt and was suspended from his neck by a thin leather strip. With a single violent tug he tore it free and lunged directly at Tommy Quinn. But before he had taken three full steps the cobblestone floor sagged, buckled, then collapsed into an invisible, though audible, subterranean river. With it went the boxes, each adding to the downward pull, until all were gone. The last sight Tommy Quinn had of Nigel Greenaway was his angry face between two raised fists, one gripping the glowing Davy lamp and the other a glinting shard of obsidian. Then he was gone, lost among the tumbling boulders and spinning boxes. Even Quinn's own bullseye torch was sent spinning down into the great pit of nothingness, leaving him dangling with nothing beneath his feet but oblivion.

'Get him out of there!' shouted Jarrett. 'Come on, I won't be happy until I see him up here.'

★ ★ ★

Half a dozen uniformed police officers from the local constabulary in three punts were spread out equally across the Kelvin, where it ran out of speed and settled down to meander gently. That was where they easily intercepted and gaffed the floating boxes and also where they found some human remains, mangled beyond recognition.

★ ★ ★

When they got back to headquarters and set about drying out the contents, Tommy Quinn and DC Russell went off to retrieve the final box from Greenaway's house.

'By the way, Superintendent Jarrett,' desk sergeant Davie Black offered cautiously, 'the CC is upstairs. He's not a happy man.'

For once, Henry Jarrett didn't particularly care how Rattray was. Now that he had reached an understanding with Elsie Maitland exactly when and how he severed all ties with the job were of no consequence. In fact, the Chief Constable might be doing him a great favour if he asked for a letter of resignation.

Jarrett knocked on the door at the top of the stairs, received a muttered response, and entered quickly.

'I believe you want to see me, sir,' he said, pre-empting whatever Rattray intended to blurt out. 'However, we do have a great deal of work in hand. All serious cases have been resolved and we have taken possession of the so-called treasure hoard. As soon as we catalogue the pieces there will be nothing to prevent the Clyde Navigation Trust from claiming the finder's fee as you originally wished.'

Chief Constable Rattray stared, open-mouthed, his proposed outburst dead at source, then slowly settled down in his chair.

'The murders?' he enquired weakly.

'At an end, sir. The perpetrator died attempting to kill an officer.'

'Good Lord.' The CC was briefly at a loss for words, but that state never continued for long. 'Let me have a full account within the hour, Jarrett. I am required to make a speech at the City Chambers tonight and it might be nice to let them know how we solved the whole thing.'

'I will do, sir. I will let you know exactly how we solved it.'

'Excellent. But then we always do, don't we? We always solve it.'

* * *

Elsie Maitland took one look at the vision on the doorstep and clasped a hand to her chest.

'Gracious me!' she exclaimed. 'What on earth has happened to you, Mr Sweetman?'

Albert Sweetman could at best be described as rumpled from head to toe. His hat, usually well brushed and jauntily angled, was no longer in evidence and his straw-coloured hair was both tousled and flecked with what looked like small pieces of vegetation. Particularly astonishing was the fact that his colourful brocade waistcoat, or a large chunk of it, now protruded from the carpet bag he gripped tightly under his left arm, revealing an even larger area of wrinkled shirt than was proper. His trousers looked for all the world as though they had been slept in and his boots were muddy and scuffed. To crown the unkempt image, he clearly had not shaved in some days.

'Oh, Mrs Maitland,' he moaned, 'you cannot begin to imagine what it feels like to be home. I have been so ill and confined to bed in some dreadful dwelling situated in the back of beyond.'

'Come inside,' the good lady encouraged, pulling him through the doorway so that she could close the door on neighbours who draw colourful conclusions from insufficient evidence. 'Now, try to make sense, Mr Sweetman. What is the nature of your illness?'

'Well,' he murmured, seemingly unconscious of the attention being paid him by the maids at the foot of the stairs and Mr McConnell at the top of them, 'I am certainly not calling into question the breakfast I had before leaving your excellent establishment.'

'I should sincerely hope not, Mr Sweet-man.'

'No, indeed, Mrs Maitland. I can only think that it must have been the pork pie I had for luncheon on the steamboat.'

'Pork?' Wilbur McConnell the quiet chemist said in an uncharacteristically loud voice. 'That can be very dangerous, sir. Not a meat I would recommend at this time of the year.'

Mrs Maitland nodded to Mr McConnell in acknowledgement of his contribution, then turned her attention once more to the dishevelled salesman.

'Do you think you could force a little food down, Mr Sweetman?' she asked sympathetically.

'I think I might, Mrs Maitland, I think I just might. Until a few hours ago I would have said otherwise, but the worst has passed and I am most decidedly on the mend.'

'Excellent. Well, if you would like to retire to your room and render yourself afresh, you will be just in time for dinner.'

By the time the junior partner of Hall & Sweetman presented himself in the dining-room, washed, shaved and with a change of all garments, Superintendent Henry Jarrett and Elliot Stainer, salaried officer of the Clyde Navigation Trust, had returned from their daily

316

duties and taken their places at their respective tables, having politely acknowledged Wilbur McConnell and, to Elsie Maitland's delight, each other.

'I will explain later,' Jarrett had whispered to his landlady in the hallway. 'All is well.'

'Wonderful,' she replied in yet quieter tones, 'just wonderful.'

The good Mr Sweetman, according to whom the consuming of food had been until a few hours earlier unthinkable, had never been one for waiting until all others lifted their spoons, and this occasion was no exception. By the time Jarrett had started his ox-tail soup, the burly salesman had already finished his and was peering forlornly at the empty bowl.

'I am most relieved to see that your appetite has returned, Mr Sweetman,' Wilbur McConnell observed, but respectfully. 'All symptoms gone now?'

'Not exactly all,' Albert Sweetman confessed, and embarked on the truth for the first time since he got back to Mrs Maitland's superior guest-house for single gentlemen at 76 Delmont Avenue. Up to this point almost every word he had uttered had been a lie in defence of dignity. To give a thoroughgoing account of what had really happened would have been unthinkable. 'I still have quite severe pains on either side of the midriff.'

'Most interesting.' McConnell frowned as he mulled over this fact. 'Tell me, Mr Sweetman, do you wear a money belt?'

'Actually, yes,' the salesman said, looking mildly abashed. 'Always have done.'

'Yes, sir, but I would venture to suggest that of late, and for some reason I cannot begin to fathom, you have given it that extra tug, perhaps on the assumption that an extra hole in the belt tongue meant increased security.'

Albert Sweetman could scarcely argue with this.

'That may well have been the case, sir,' he said, ignoring Jarrett's broad grin. The damned man was enjoying his suffering, though God alone knew why. He had never done him any harm. 'In fact, now that you mention it, it is very much the case.'

'And are you still wearing it?'

'I'm afraid so. Force of habit, you see.'

'Then I would suggest that you remove it immediately. I will prepare some green liniment which you must rub onto the affected areas. It is a tiny quantity of henbane and chloroform, plus some wintergreen and mineral oil.'

'Liniment?' Sweetman echoed. 'Is it serious, Mr McConnell?'

'Oh, dear no. You merely have the ladies' complaint, Mr Sweetman. It is called corset pain.'

Conscious of the fact that Jarrett's shoulders were heaving and his spoon shaking, even though no actual sounds were coming from that quarter, Albert Sweetman tugged open the twin buckle straps of his money belt and dragged the heavy item out through his unbuttoned shirt. Then he placed it on the floor beneath his chair and plonked both booted feet firmly on it.

If the other diners were conscious of this act of blatant distrust, Jeannie Craig was not. She wheeled her trolley across the large cherry-red carpet like someone possessed, then in a gesture that would have done credit to a pickpocket, whisked away Sweetman's empty bowl and replaced it with a large platter of stewed steak and mixed vegetables.

Henry Jarrett stole a quick glance at Elsie Maitland, hovering as always by the door, and received a knowing smile in return. Someone, the look confirmed, was out to prove her worth and long may she continue.

We do hope that you have enjoyed reading this large print book.

Did you know that all of our titles are available for purchase?

We publish a wide range of high quality large print books including:
**Romances, Mysteries, Classics
General Fiction
Non Fiction and Westerns**

Special interest titles available in large print are:
**The Little Oxford Dictionary
Music Book
Song Book
Hymn Book
Service Book**

Also available from us courtesy of Oxford University Press:
**Young Readers' Dictionary
(large print edition)
Young Readers' Thesaurus
(large print edition)**

For further information or a free brochure, please contact us at:
**Ulverscroft Large Print Books Ltd.,
The Green, Bradgate Road, Anstey,
Leicester, LE7 7FU, England.
Tel:** (00 44) **0116 236 4325**
Fax: (00 44) **0116 234 0205**

Other titles published by
The House of Ulverscroft:

AVENGING THE DEAD

Guy Fraser

1863. Superintendent Henry Jarrett, chief of the detective department at Glasgow Central, begins to investigate a forgery scandal, involving the Union Bank . . . but then the murders begin. Each killing is claimed by a mysterious letter-writer calling himself the Scythe, who declares himself to be a righter of wrongs. The writer is seemingly in possession of facts known only to the detectives. Jarrett is troubled — the lady in his life seems far too interested in a dashing sea captain — and the most recent murder is not accompanied by the usual letter. Now it seems that Jarrett has two killers to contend with . . .

A PLAGUE OF LIONS

Guy Fraser

1863. Superintendent Henry Jarrett, formerly of the Hong Kong police and now Chief of the Detective Department at Glasgow Central, is comfortably ensconced in Elsie Maitland's superior guest house for single gentlemen. However, the tranquillity is short-lived when a major bank robbery calls for the attention of Jarrett, Inspector Charlie Grant and Sergeant Tommy Quinn. Then, the undermanned department has a series of gory murders, an attacker who lies in wait for maids on their night off, and a cold-blooded poisoner. Stretched to breaking point, they can well do without the activities of a confidence trickster and his loyal assistant . . .